WARNING: FALLING ROCKS

Abruptly, Kip, the Hardys' guide, stopped. They were in a canyon, its walls looming high on either side. "It gets really narrow in through here," Kip said. "We'll have to go single file."

"There isn't any chance of getting stuck, is there?" Joe asked with a smile.

Kip laughed. "I've never seen it happen." He led the way through the canyon, followed by the Hardys. Soon the walls were so close that Kip had to take off his pack, turn sideways, and sidle through.

Frank could just see Kip through the sliver of light let in by the narrow passage. He took a deep breath and squeezed his way through.

As Frank emerged on the other side, he thought he heard a rumbling sound above. He looked up and saw a huge boulder rolling down the sheer rock wall. It was headed straight for Joe, who was struggling to pull himself out of the narrow passageway.

"Avalanche!" Frank yelled as Kip covered his head with his arms. "Get out of there, Joe!"

Books in THE HARDY BOYS CASEFILES™ Series

Available from ARCHWAY Paperbacks

THE HARDY BOYS

CASEFILES™

NO. 120

SURVIVAL OF THE FITTEST

FRANKLIN W. DIXON

AN ARCHWAY PAPERBACK
Published by POCKET BOOKS
New York London Toronto Sydney Tokyo Singapore

This book is a work of fiction. Names, characters, places and incidents are products of the author's imagination or are used fictiously. Any resemblance to actual events or locales or persons, living or dead, is entirely coincidental.

AN ARCHWAY PAPERBACK *Original*

An Archway Paperback published by
POCKET BOOKS, a division of Simon & Schuster Inc.
1230 Avenue of the Americas, New York, NY 10020

Copyright © 1997 by Simon & Schuster Inc.
Produced by Mega-Books, Inc.

ISBN: 0-671-56120-0

First Archway Paperback printing February 1997

10 9 8 7 6 5 4 3 2 1

THE HARDY BOYS, AN ARCHWAY PAPERBACK and colophon are registered trademarks of Simon & Schuster Inc.

THE HARDY BOYS CASEFILES is a trademark of Simon & Schuster Inc.

Cover photograph from "The Hardy Boys" Series © 1995 Nelvana Limited/Marathon Productions S.A. All rights reserved.

Logo design TM & © 1995 by Nelvana Limited. All rights reserved.

Printed in the U.S.A.

IL 6+

SURVIVAL OF THE FITTEST

Chapter

1

"WELL, IT'S DEFINITELY NOT BAYPORT," Joe Hardy said, taking in the spectacular jagged red rocks jutting up to pierce the brilliant blue sky.

Frank Hardy eased his six-foot-one frame out of the 4×4 and joined his younger brother at the overlook. The warm air of Moab, Utah, blew softly in his face as he admired the browns and reds of the rocky landscape, which was cut by canyons stretching as far as he could see. The town itself was nestled below in the Colorado River Valley, where the only trees in the entire vista were in spring bloom.

"Whoa," Frank said.

A lean young man with curly brown hair stepped out from the far side of the green four-wheeler.

"You city folk are all the same," he said with a chuckle. "One look at this view and you can't say anything halfway intelligent."

Frank smiled at his friend Kip Coles. "I'll leave the talking to Joe," he said. "I'm happy just to look."

Kip had just picked up the Hardys at the airport to begin their week-long vacation in southeastern Utah. On the way into town, he pulled over to show them his favorite view. Frank and Joe were pumped to spend their spring break exploring the desert and mountains in and around nearby Canyonlands National Park.

Frank and Joe had met Kip a couple of years earlier when he had visited an uncle in Bayport who was a client of their father, Fenton. Now the Hardys had accepted Kip's invitation to join him in Moab, where another uncle ran a tour business called ExploreUtah.

"So what are we waiting for?" Joe asked, hopping back into Kip's truck. "Let's hit the canyons."

"I can see Joe's just as patient as ever," Kip said with a laugh. "Are you ready, Frank?"

Frank took one last look at the awesome panorama, nodded, and climbed back in for the short ride into Moab. Even though it was obvious they were brothers, Frank and Joe had completely different personalities. Frank, an inch taller, with brown hair and a lean, muscular build, was often quiet and thoughtful, whereas Joe, with blond hair and built like a running back, was impulsive and always ready to act—sometimes too fast, Frank thought.

"First we'll head for the office to pick up our equipment," Kip said after he found a parking space just off Moab's bustling main street.

"I think we may need a refresher course in climbing, too," Frank added. "It's been a while."

Kip nodded, tucking his keys in his shorts pocket. "I mapped out a nice trip for the week," he said. "There's a lot of variety in the terrain and scenery. I figured our first leg could be some hiking and basic climbing in Canyonlands so you guys can ease back into it."

"Sounds good," Frank said.

Kip led the Hardys into a small brick building. There was a big bold ExploreUtah sign on the glass door they pushed through. Inside were a couple of desks with chairs, a few filing cabinets, and bags and boxes packed with food and camping gear. Frank assumed these were for their trip. The walls were covered with topographical maps and enlarged photographs of some stunning rock and canyon formations.

A man, who appeared to be in his midforties, with short, graying hair and a tanned, lined face, sat behind one desk, speaking into the phone. He waved at Kip and the Hardys.

"That's Uncle Ted," Kip said in a low voice. Frank and Joe waved back at Ted Coles.

"How long have you worked with your uncle?" Joe asked.

"He started letting me tag along on trips when I was about thirteen," Kip said. "Eventually I got to lead sections of a tour. Now I've started to take out a few clients on my own."

"Like us," Frank said.

Kip shook his head as he lifted a backpack crammed with gear. "Nah, you guys aren't clients, you're more like guinea pigs," he said with a wink.

Frank and Joe each picked up a pack and followed Kip back to his four-by-four. Frank had just stepped onto the sidewalk when a booming voice from down the street yelled out, "Going back out there to make another mess? Tear things up with that Jeep of yours? I see you've got some help."

Frank looked up to see an older bearded man in jeans, cowboy boots, and a Stetson stride down the sidewalk toward them. He was pointing at Kip, squinting, his expression full of anger.

"Oh, man," Kip muttered.

"Looks like you bused in some more out-of-towners to trample all over our land again," the old cowboy said, spitting a thick stream of tobacco juice from between his two front teeth.

"I don't believe we've met, and I don't like

4

your tone," Joe said, dropping his pack and squaring his shoulders to the man. "Where I come from strangers don't—"

Kip held up his hand. "It's okay, Joe. Mr. Hyrum here isn't a stranger."

Hyrum let out a guffaw. "And I ain't no friend either. Kip Coles, both you and your uncle know where I stand, and I represent plenty of folks in this town. You can't fool us with all your 'eco-friendly' stuff. We know you're recruiting tourists. You're ruining this place and making plenty of money doing it. We know you're stealing fossils, arrowheads, and anything else you can get your hands on and selling 'em for cash. You can't hide it."

Suddenly Hyrum stepped up to Frank and Joe and stuck a finger in Joe's face. "And you listen to me. I'll be watching you. One false move and I'll have you arrested."

"And you listen to me, Mr. Hyrum," Joe said, bringing his face to within inches of Hyrum's. "I don't like being threatened. And I don't like people talking to my friends like that either."

Frank grabbed Joe's arm and slowly pulled him back. At the same time Kip shook his head and stepped in between Joe and Hyrum. "It's not worth it, Joe," he said. "Hyrum and his cronies don't have anything better to do than annoy the legitimate businesses in this town."

"Legitimate?" Hyrum said. "That ain't even funny. You boys—"

Kip cut him off. "Yeah, you heard me—legitimate. And if you keep up the threats, I'll call the police, just like my uncle did." He turned his back on the man, walked to the truck, and hoisted the packs into the rear cargo area.

Hyrum resettled his hat and stalked up to Kip. Frank glanced from Kip to Hyrum, ready for Hyrum to explode.

Instead, Hyrum just leaned in close to Kip's ear. "Don't forget, Kippy," he said almost in a whisper, "I'm like a hawk. I can wait and watch for hours before I move in for the kill." With that he strode away, and Kip motioned for Frank and Joe to follow him back inside ExploreUtah.

"What's this about stealing fossils and arrowheads?" Frank asked.

Before Kip could answer, Ted Coles hung up the phone and said, "Kip, did I hear Russ Hyrum out there?"

"Yeah," Kip said. "Frank and Joe just got the usual earful."

Ted Coles shook his head and sighed. "You know, if Hyrum wasn't so thick-headed, he could be interesting." He stood up to shake hands with the Hardys. "I'm Kip's uncle Ted. I guess we were introduced while I was on the phone. You must be the Hardys."

Frank and Joe shook Ted's hand. "Hyrum was

6

a rancher around here for years," he continued. "Every time the environmentalists tried to have land designated as protected wilderness, he fought it. He said they were just trying to put ranchers like him out of business. Now he wants to put *us* out of business."

"He's right to be concerned," Kip said. "But that doesn't mean you run around accusing innocent people of stealing Indian artifacts or wrecking the environment." He turned to Frank and Joe. "We're very careful about making sure our clients use the land properly."

"Have there really been any thefts?" Frank asked.

Ted Coles nodded. "Unfortunately, some people just take whatever they find. Some even scribble graffiti on the ancient rock carvings or petroglyphs."

"And Hyrum's blaming it on you?" Joe said.

Coles sat back in his chair and nodded. "He's accosted us on the street, ranted about us to the town officials, even tried to scare away our clients."

"Any help from the police?" Frank asked.

Coles shrugged. "They can't do much—just warn him. I mentioned it to them once. But this is a small town, and we're going to have to live with each other. I'd like to be able to work it out with Hyrum man to man."

Frank nodded, but he understood that Hyrum

7

probably wasn't the type of person to reason with.

"Hey, guys, we're not here to discuss local politics," Kip said. He looked at his watch. "We've got some hiking and climbing to do."

"Great," Joe said, picking up an armful of water bottles. The three teenagers packed the rest of the equipment into the truck and said goodbye to Kip's uncle Ted, who was leaving on his own trip the next morning.

The hour-long drive to Canyonlands National Park went quickly because there was so much to see and do. Frank and Joe stared out the windows at the Colorado River Valley as it changed from parched desert to wildly shaped canyons. As they drove, Kip told them about the hikes he had planned for the next few days, talking them through a map Frank had unfolded on his lap. Joe went through the backpacks, double-checking the water, food, camping, and climbing supplies.

Finally Kip pulled off the main road onto a well-used dirt road lined with scraggly brush, tamarisk shrubs with beautiful feathery flowers, and jagged rocks. The road dead-ended in a small clearing where they parked. The three pulled on their packs and attached their climbing gear after which Kip led them through thick underbrush. He explained that this was the start of one of the many little-used trails in over 100,000 acres of land in Canyonlands National Park.

As Frank and Joe followed Kip, up and north and west by Frank's compass, the terrain changed. The vegetation became more sparse, and the rock formations became more rugged. Frank looked up and saw that they were reaching the crest of a mesa. Miles of square and jagged rocks spread out before him, with chasms and crevices formed between their sides.

They walked along the flat rockface until it abruptly dropped off. Kip stopped at the edge, near a single pine tree that seemed to be growing right out of the rock. Frank and Joe joined him, peering down the narrow crack between two rock formations.

"All right," Joe said, wiping the sweat from his face with his T-shirt. "This looks like a slot canyon."

"That's right," Kip said. "Some of them are up to one hundred feet deep and so narrow you can barely squeeze through them."

"I read about them," Frank said, recalling the geology book he'd read on the four-and-a-half-hour flight from the East Coast. The book explained how millions of years of water running through the canyons had carved out these deep crevices.

"We'll be dropping down by rope," Kip said. "At the bottom, it opens up to a much wider sandy stretch. Then we have a five-mile hike back up to the top, where our gear is." Frank nodded and knelt at the edge of the rock, trying to get his bearings before the descent.

Meanwhile, Joe attached a harness with a climbing rope to his waist, cinching the other end of the rope to an anchor rope that was attached to a bolt permanently secured in the tree. "Okay, slowpokes," he said. "See you at the bottom."

"Hang on, Joe," Frank said, standing up. "We need to check each other's positions, and—" Joe had released his grip and was already sliding down into the slot canyon.

Frank stopped and stared at Kip. "Forget it," he said. "Joe's been waiting too long for this."

Kip didn't answer. Bent over the tree where Joe had attached his rope, he was frowning.

"What is it?" Frank asked, suddenly aware of how quiet it was.

"This anchor rope—it's totally frayed. One more pull, and it's likely to snap."

Chapter

2

"Hey, Joe," Frank yelled, his voice echoing eerily through the slot canyon.

"Hurry up, guys," Joe's voice called up. "I'm way ahead of you."

Frank turned to Kip. "We can't pull him up," he said. "He's too far down."

Kip had already roped up, latching on his harness with quick, efficient movements. "Strap in," he said to Frank, his voice dry against the canyon wind. "We have to get down there quick."

Frank nodded, hooking up his own climbing rope and checking the anchor bolt on the tree in one swift motion. As he did, he glanced at the frayed rope that was still holding Joe. Even if Joe was already halfway down when that rope snapped it would be at least a fifty-foot fall, which meant broken bones—at best.

Kip backed over the edge of the rockface, holding the rope in front of him as he checked behind himself for Joe. Then Frank slipped over, too, gripping his rope.

"It's about time," Joe said as soon as he saw them sliding down from above. "I thought I'd be squeezing through here all by myself."

"Hold up, Joe," Frank said. "There's a problem with your rope." He and Kip slid down and pulled even with Joe within seconds. Frank bumped up against the rock wall behind him. The three of them were in a space made for one comfortably, and it was hard not to feel claustrophobic.

"What's wrong?" Joe asked, stopping his descent while Frank and Kip tucked themselves slightly under and beside him. Frank tried to steady himself by bracing his feet against the rock, and Kip did the same thing on the other side of Joe.

"Your anchor rope's frayed," Frank said. "We've got to get you off it right away." The three of them hung motionless.

"Okay," Joe said. "Just a second and I can—" As he shifted slightly to try to wedge himself in the crevice, the rope snapped.

Kip grabbed Joe by the armpits and yelled, "Hang on!" as Joe fell into Frank. Joe caught hold of Frank's shirt with one hand and braced himself against the rockface with the other. Frank grabbed Joe around the waist, and the three of them swayed in the breeze as one unit about sixty-five feet above the sandy canyon floor.

"Whoa," Joe said, glancing down but careful not to lower his head or shift his weight. "That was close."

"We've got you," Frank said quietly. He tried to sound confident, but he was straining against Joe's weight.

"Just hang on, and we'll bring you down," Kip grunted, glancing down.

Without another word, the three began rappeling down the rockface. Frank and Kip watched each other and timed their movements until they found a slow rhythm together. With the weight of three bodies, they had to be extra careful to keep their bouncing to a minimum.

Frank could feel his muscles burn as he glanced up at his own rope, hoping it was more secure than Joe's had been.

Kip's voice broke the silence. "Okay, easy," he said, his voice strained from his concentrated effort. "Just about forty feet more."

The fissure opened up, and they could push off in front of them with bigger motions. Frank and Kip relaxed their grips on the ropes, and the threesome picked up some speed.

After three more pushes, Frank could feel the sandy bottom of the canyon underneath his right foot. He let go, and the three of them collapsed in a heap on the sand, breathing heavily. Frank's shirt was wet with sweat, and his hands, shoulders, and back quivered with fatigue.

After a few seconds Joe stood and gazed up at the slot canyon that seemed to narrow to a slit at the top. "Thanks, guys," he said. "So what happened? I thought my ropes were secure."

Kip sat in the sand, his elbows on his knees. "They were, but the anchor was frayed." He shook his head. "It never should have been left there."

"Maybe if you hadn't been in such a hurry, Joe . . ." Frank muttered almost to himself.

"Okay," Joe said. "Good point, but the question is, how did the anchor get that way?"

Kip shrugged as he stood up and readjusted his small pack. "Sometimes they just dry out when they're in the sun for too long," he said. "You have to be careful about those old ones. We can check it out later." Frank just nodded, his eyes shifting around the canyon.

"Well, I don't know how you guys feel, but that was a nice warmup for me," Joe said, a smile pulling at the corners of his mouth. "You aren't tired, are you?"

"Try hauling your dead weight down sixty-five feet," Frank said as he threw a handful of sand at his brother.

Kip unfolded a detailed map and showed them

the winding trail they would take back up through the canyon. They each had a few slugs of water from their canteens, then began the trek.

"Check out these colors," Joe said, gazing at the strange rock shapes in shades of red, orange, and brown.

"It took Mother Nature millions of years to carve this, and I think it's the most beautiful terrain in America," Kip said. "Of course, I might be a little biased because it's right in my own backyard."

As he reached the top of the canyon, Joe could tell that Frank had switched into detective mode. His brother stood silently, examining the gnarled old tree where their ropes were anchored. Kip and Joe joined him.

"Look at this anchor rope," Kip said as he examined the end of Joe's broken one.

Frank fingered the frayed piece of blue nylon that was tied into the ring. "It could have been done deliberately," he said.

Joe scowled. "Why would anyone do it? And how would he know who'd use it next?"

Frank stood up and shook his head. "I just keep hearing Russ Hyrum's voice and wondering if he really wants to make good on his threats."

"How would he know we'd come here?" Joe asked.

"This is one of my favorite spots," Kip explained. "Most people around town would know.

Take a good look at this anchor, Joe. It's just plain dried out. Next time, don't forget to check *all* your ropes before you hop over the edge."

Joe agreed while Frank glanced around the empty mesa. He couldn't completely shake the feeling that this was more than just an accident. "Let's just stay watchful and keep an eye out for trouble."

"Good idea," Kip said, and began gathering up the climbing gear. "And now it's about time we made camp." The late afternoon sun was low behind the western ridges. "I have a great place in mind. It's close to where we parked and right beside a creek where we can catch our dinner. I brought along some fishing poles."

Joe was taking a long drink from his canteen, but the word *fishing* caught his attention. "Excellent," he said. "Frank's been riding me about not knowing how to fly-fish for years. Can you give me a lesson, Kip?"

Kip shrugged. "All it takes is patience and a good wrist."

"Then forget Joe," Frank said.

Kip laughed as he lifted his pack and led the Hardys back down the trail. About halfway down he turned and headed off the trail. Within half an hour, they came to an area of broken rock, cut through by a rippling creek. Trees and small scrub brush grew along its banks, which were made of stratified rock instead of dirt and moss.

Frank sat down on a boulder near the creek to take a breather, but Joe grabbed Kip before he could join Frank. "Let's get those poles and do some fishing," he said.

"I thought we might want to set up camp first," Kip said.

"Remember what Kip said about patience, Joe?" Frank asked. "But you go ahead and start fishing. I'll unpack and get some food started—just in case the fish aren't biting," he added.

About an hour later Frank was stirring the sauce for spaghetti over a small cookstove under a sky streaked with the orange, purple, and red of a dying sunset. He looked up as Kip and Joe came lumbering into the campsite.

"You'd better be bringing some fresh trout," he called out.

Kip approached Frank, his face twisted in a grimace. "Not really," he said. Joe came up behind Kip, and Frank saw the frustration on his brother's face. "But we sure were close, weren't we, Joe?"

Now Frank could see Kip was trying hard not to laugh.

"Well, sometimes they're just not biting," Frank said.

"I wouldn't know," Joe said. "I couldn't even cast without catching the stupid line on something. A tree, something in the creek, Kip's shirt—"

"Kip's shirt?" Frank said. "Any injuries?"

Kip let out a laugh. "No, but that was a pretty sorry exhibition of fly casting, Joe. I've never seen anything like it. I thought you were going to flip me in the creek."

"Maybe you ought to try fishing with a spear next time, Joe," Frank said.

"Not with me around," Kip said.

Joe grinned and shook his head. "Okay, that's enough, you two. Now I hope there's something cooking because I'm starved."

"Pasta à la Hardy," Frank said. "Grab a plate. There's plenty."

Kip and Joe took apart their portable fishing poles, got plates, and piled them high with Frank's spaghetti. They all sat on the ground, perching their plates on their knees. For a few minutes the only other sound was that of the running creek as the three hungry teens attacked their food. Frank smiled, thinking how much better even the simplest dish tasted outdoors as the stars came out in the night sky.

After he'd finished, Kip told them that in the morning they'd be heading for some canyons just west of the national park. There would be plenty of hiking and rock climbing. He also planned to show them some petroglyphs, and maybe they'd even come across a few fossils.

After cleaning up, they stored the food and cooking equipment in Kip's truck, which he'd moved closer to their campsite. Then they pitched two tents—one for Kip and one for Frank and Joe.

"I don't know about you guys, but I'm beat," Joe announced when they were done.

"I guess all that fishing wore you out," Kip said.

Joe leveled a gaze at him. "Hey, don't you start in on that again. I get enough of that from him," he said, jerking his thumb toward Frank.

Kip laughed and waved good night as he crawled into his tent. Within minutes, Frank and Joe had settled in their sleeping bags and drifted off to sleep.

Frank dreamed about a crunching noise, the noise their feet had made all afternoon as they hiked. He rolled over, trying to shake the dream loose. Then he realized it wasn't a dream. The crunching sound was real, and it was coming from just outside his tent.

Blinking his eyes open, Frank silently slipped out of his sleeping bag. He could hear Joe's heavy breathing next to him.

Without a sound, he poked his head through the tent flap, squinting into the darkness. His eyes darted to a figure standing just a few feet from him. It was Kip.

Kip was pressed up against a large boulder next to his tent. His eyes caught Frank's, and he put an index finger to his lips, signaling Frank to keep quiet. Then he moved the finger to a pointing position.

Frank's eyes followed the finger over to where Kip's truck was parked. He heard the crunching sound again. A raccoon? No. As his eyes adjusted, Frank could make out two figures bent over the passenger door of the truck, working on the window frame. Someone was trying to break in.

Chapter 3

FRANK'S EYES DARTED BACK to Kip, who was still watching the two figures intently from behind his rock.

Frank pulled his head back in the tent and leaned over Joe, shaking him. "Joe," he whispered. Joe moved, but Frank had to shake him again before Joe opened his eyes.

"Shh," Frank said, pointing outside.

Joe squinted, trying to squeeze the sleep out of his eyes. He sat up, nodded, slipped out of his sleeping bag, and crawled to the tent opening. He peeked through and then pulled his head back, giving Frank the thumbs-up signal indicating that he had seen the intruders.

"Let's grab them before they pick the lock,"

Frank said in a whisper. He and Joe silently pulled on their sneakers. Then, with Frank leading the way, they crawled through the tent opening.

Out of the corner of his eye, Frank saw Kip still pressed up against the boulder. About twenty feet ahead, the two figures were still concentrating on the door of the truck. Frank stopped moving forward when he saw one of them turn his head and look around nervously. Frank could tell he was a young man, but in the darkness, he couldn't see much else.

Frank crept toward the back of the truck, and he and Joe hid in the brush there.

Suddenly one of the two figures turned his head sharply, staring right at Frank. The young man's eyes were wide with terror.

Frank charged immediately with Joe just behind him. The Hardys grabbed both intruders and within seconds had wrestled them to the ground.

"Hey, man, take it easy!" the guy under Frank said. Frank glanced up and saw Kip come crashing through the underbrush with a flashlight.

In the beam from Kip's light, Frank found himself staring down at a baby-faced, blond-haired kid about sixteen years old, the expression on his face a mixture of shock and guilt.

"All right, I give up. Get off me," someone yelled behind Frank. He turned to see Joe sitting on top of a dark-haired young man, his knee pressed against the intruder's chest.

"I don't think so," Joe said. "Not until we talk about what you and your friend were doing breaking into our truck."

Kip turned his flashlight beam onto the young man's face. His dark hair was dirty and hung in long strands over his face. He had on jeans and a T-shirt, and more than anything, Frank thought, he looked tired.

When the young man didn't say anything, Kip shone the flashlight onto the passenger door of his truck. "If there's even a scratch," he muttered, "you two are going to—"

"There's no damage," the blond kid said nervously, his voice high and clear in the quiet of the night. Frank stared down at him, just noticing how skinny he was. "We weren't going to do anything. We just wanted to see if you had some food or water."

"Food or water?" Kip said. "Where's yours?"

The blond teen just glanced at his dark-haired companion, who said, "We ran out. We were headed back to our camp, and we kind of got lost."

"We haven't had anything to eat for twenty-four hours," the blond kid added. Frank stared down at him. He sure looked hungry. These kids look desperate, more like runaways than lost campers, Frank thought.

"You left your camp with only the clothes on your back?" Kip said. "No compass? No water?" He looked them over. "Are you from around here?"

With the flashlight beam in their eyes, both teens looked away, not answering. Finally, the blond kid said, "I'm Jeremy, and this is Jorge. We just—"

"We just got off track a little," Jorge said, sounding a little more confident. "Look, man, we're sorry about trying to break into your truck. We didn't want to wake anybody or startle them. I swear, all we wanted was some food or water, just something until we could get back to our camp."

"Where's that?" Joe asked.

"Ah, it's a little south of here," Jorge said. "We'll find it in the daylight. It just got dark a little quicker than we thought." He tried to smile, and Joe stole a glance at Frank. They were both wondering what the real story was.

Kip sighed. "You guys have got to be careful out here," Kip said. "The weather can turn on you in a minute, and it's easy to lose your bearings." He paused, then added, "We can give you some food and water to tide you over."

Both Jeremy and Jorge looked up. "Hey, thanks," Jorge said. "We really appreciate that."

"Thanks a lot," Jeremy added.

Kip went around and opened the back of his

truck. Joe and Frank let the two teens up off the ground, but Joe still eyed them suspiciously.

"How long were you planning on staying in the park?" Frank asked.

Jeremy's eyes met the ground again, and Jorge answered, "That's hard to tell. We're sort of playing it by ear."

Kip closed the back of the truck and came around with a water bottle, a few energy bars, and a plastic big filled with dry cereal. "This should do it," he said as the boys gratefully took the food. "Now, why don't you tell me exactly where you need to go, and I'll give you the shortest route?"

But the two had already backed away from the truck and now were jogging away from the camp.

"Thanks again," Jorge called over his shoulder.

"Hey, wait—" Joe yelled, his voice echoing off the canyon walls around them.

The two figures dashed upstream, the crunching sound of their feet quickly fading into the darkness.

Kip's flashlight made a small circle of light on the rocky ground. The three of them stood around in silence, listening to the rippling of the creek.

"Well, that was weird," Joe finally said.

Frank nodded. "More than weird. I don't like it. Who leaves a campsite without a pack and with no sense of where they're going?"

Kip had been staring off in the direction the two teens had fled. Now he turned to Frank and Joe. "You'd be surprised," he said. "People see pictures of this scenery and think they can just come out to see it. They forget that this isn't a controlled environment, that you have to be prepared for some rough terrain and fickle weather.

"Last year two mountain bikers died just seven miles outside of Moab. They got completely turned around in the canyons, hopelessly lost. They didn't have any food, water, or maps. You can freeze to death out here at night even at this time of year."

The three of them were silent for a moment. Then Joe said, "Those two could be in real trouble then. They looked completely worn out."

Frank nodded. "They weren't exactly eager to answer any questions either."

"I wonder if they could be from a wilderness survival program," Kip said. "They send the kids out in this area."

"What's that?" Joe asked.

"Parents put their out-of-control teens in a program to learn survival skills for maybe a few weeks," Kip said. "It's supposed to help them pull their lives together."

"I've read about those programs," Frank said. "A group of kids are taken out to the middle of nowhere and have to learn to use their skills and common sense to work together to survive."

"They get food and water and survival lessons," Kip said. "There are trained leaders with them, but the kids are supposed to do everything on their own. It's to help build self-esteem and discipline."

"Some of the programs work really well," Frank said. "Some of them don't."

"The one that's around here is called Right Directions," Kip said. "There have been some complaints about it. There were three kids who said they weren't supervised and ran out of food and water right away. They got lost and would have starved to death if a rescue team hadn't found them. They said the experience was more like torture than a wilderness outing."

"So you think Jeremy and Jorge are in that program?" Frank asked.

Kip nodded slowly. "Seems likely. It would explain why they're wandering around with no food or water and why they didn't want to tell us anything about their camp."

Frank looked up at the star-filled night sky. From the way Jeremy and Jorge were acting, he thought Kip was probably right—and he was curious to find out more.

It seemed to Joe as if he had just gotten comfortable in his sleeping bag when the sunlight began flooding in through the thin nylon of the tent. He groaned. "It can't be morning already."

Frank didn't answer; Joe rolled over to discover he was alone in the tent. He crawled out from his sleeping bag and then through the tent flap.

"Hey, it's about time," Frank said. He and Kip were sitting on some rocks, each finishing a bowl of oatmeal. Joe could smell coffee, and he saw that Kip's tent had already been neatly taken down and his supplies packed.

Joe squinted in the sunlight. "Did you guys ever go back to sleep last night?" he said.

Kip chuckled. "Sure. But last night ended a long time ago."

Joe stretched and yawned. "It sure doesn't feel like it."

"Grab some food so we can hit the road," Frank said. "Kip wants to show us those petroglyphs."

Joe nodded, still groggy. "All right, all right. But they've been there for what—ten thousand years? I don't think they're going anywhere in the next few hours."

Frank shook his head. "And neither are we if we have to wait for you."

Joe disappeared into the tent again. It took him only a few minutes to dress and eat, and then he and Frank took down their tent. After storing the supplies in the truck, the three set off, making their way in and out of some small canyons.

As the sun rose higher in the sky, Kip led the Hardys down a dry, narrow stretch of land flanked by reddish brown rock cliffs. They rounded a curve, and Kip ducked behind a sharp outcropping of rocks. Frank and Joe followed, crowding into the small passageway near the cliff. Kip pointed up at the cliff face, moving his head so his shadow wouldn't block the light hitting the cliff.

"There they are," Joe said, following Kip's hand as it pointed to a series of carvings in the stone.

Kip smiled. "This is one of my favorite places. They're really out of the way so they're safe from graffiti."

Frank stared at the cliff face, piecing together the simple lines, curves, and swirls that had been carved into the stone by ancient people. A few appeared to be bighorn sheep, while others looked like stick figures representing humans. The composition of the rock and the weathering it had withstood made interesting color variations throughout the markings. Kip, Frank, and Joe stood and enjoyed the mysterious beauty of the ancient artwork for several minutes.

They were quiet as they stepped out of the small passageway in awe of the images carved so long ago.

"Keep your eyes peeled," Kip said as they continued hiking. "My uncle claims there are still arrowheads in this area. I haven't seen any but he swears it's true."

"Great," Joe said, stepping ahead of the other two and staring down the dry stretch ahead of them. It was a flat, sandy area extending several hundred yards in front of them, broken up only by an array of miniature castlelike rock formations.

All at once Joe stopped and squinted. He ran a few steps ahead and then pointed between two rocks. "Hey," he said, turning to Kip and Frank, "I think that's Jorge and Jeremy."

Frank ran up to Joe. Maybe 150 yards ahead, a figure lay sprawled on the ground. It looked like the young, blond-haired teen, Jeremy. The other teen, Jorge, was standing over him.

Joe took off in their direction, with Frank on his heels. In the same instant Jorge looked up and saw the two of them. After grabbing a water bottle off the ground, he spun around and took off.

"I got him!" Joe yelled to Frank, veering off after Jorge.

Frank and Kip scrambled over to where Jeremy lay. The teen had a large gash in his skull, in the hairline just over the right side of his forehead. His T-shirt was torn open, and there were deep purplish bruises on his skinny chest. He groaned and started coughing. There was a trickle of blood at the corner of his mouth. Frank checked the boy's pulse. It was weak, and his skin was cold and clammy.

"He's in bad shape," Frank said. "Probably going into shock. We've got to get him some help quick."

Chapter

4

KIP STARED AT THE BATTERED BODY of the teen they knew as Jeremy as Frank checked the boy's head wound. He appeared to have lost a fair amount of blood but wasn't bleeding heavily now. Frank pulled a handkerchief out of his pocket and dabbed the flow. Jeremy twisted and groaned.

"Kip," Frank said. "What about your cellular phone? Do you have it?"

Kip snapped to attention. "Right—the phone." He shrugged off his pack and pulled out a small portable phone. "I'm going to call the Bureau of Land Management. They're closest."

While Kip punched in the numbers, Frank bent down to Jeremy. The teen's eyelids were half shut, and he appeared to be unconscious. Frank put his ear to Jeremy's mouth; his breathing was shallow.

"That's right," Frank heard Kip say. "We're right outside the Vista Canyon. The victim's unconscious with a head wound."

Kip clicked off the telephone. "Okay, they're sending a four-wheel-drive truck and a helicopter. We need to move Jeremy to a bigger clearing so the chopper can land to pick him up."

Frank and Kip both turned back to Jeremy. "We've got to be really careful moving him," Frank said. He glanced around, his mind racing to figure out a way to get Jeremy to a more open area.

Frank turned to Kip. "How about those portable fishing poles?" he asked.

Kip nodded. "They're in my pack."

"Great," Frank said. "If we unzip both our packs and lay them out flat, then hold them firm on either side with the poles, we can make a litter to carry him on."

"Let's do it," Kip said, grabbing his thick black waterproof pack and emptying it of its contents.

Frank pulled off his smaller pack and did the same thing. Then they laid the packs flat on the ground, side by side, and used the duct tape Kip had in his pack to hold them together. Kip snapped together the lengths of fishing poles, and he and Frank taped them to the packs.

The desert sun was high in the sky, and Frank had to stop repeatedly to wipe the sweat from the back of his neck. He and Kip positioned themselves on either side of Jeremy, gently wedging their hands under the teen's slim frame.

"Okay, Jeremy, just relax," Frank murmured before nodding to Kip to lift the kid and slide him onto their makeshift stretcher. The teen's face tightened, and another trickle of blood slipped out of the corner of his mouth.

After covering Jeremy with their windbreakers, Frank and Kip carried him to an open area about fifty yards away. Jeremy's legs hung down over the floppy, pack stretcher, and his rear end sagged in the middle. But Frank and Kip managed to hold it together long enough to make it to the clearing, where they gingerly laid him on the ground.

Kip straightened up, breathing hard. "I'll get our things," he said.

Frank stood over Jeremy. "Just a few more minutes," he said to the teen. Then he heard the sound of running footsteps. He turned, expecting to see Kip. Instead, Joe was jogging into the clearing.

Joe pulled up to Frank, stopped, and bent over, panting. When he straightened up, he shook his head. "Couldn't catch him," he said. He gestured behind him. "Over by that big rock with the petroglyphs there's a whole series of little canyons.

He ran in there, and I lost him." Joe glanced back at Jeremy, bruised and bleeding. "What do you want to bet Jorge did that to him?"

Frank squatted over Jeremy, shading the teen's face from the sun. "Jeremy, can you hear me?" he asked. "Can you tell us what happened?"

He waited for a response, but Jeremy just wagged his head back and forth, his eyes still closed.

"Can you nod?" Frank asked. "Can you just tell me if you hear me?" Still there was no response.

Joe squatted down next to his brother. "He must have been hit pretty hard," he said. "How are we going to get him out of here?"

"Kip called the Bureau of Land Management on his cell phone," Frank said. "Let's hope they find us."

Kip came back with his arms full of the contents from his and Frank's backpacks. As he set them on the ground, Frank said, "Do you have a flare or any reflective material?"

Kip glanced up and nodded. "I have some stove heat reflectors in the truck. We can spread a few of them around and send out some signals for the chopper."

Frank nodded toward Jeremy. "Let's do it. He's not getting any better, so we don't want them to waste time looking for us."

Kip rummaged through his supplies and found

his first aid kit. He took out a large sterile pad-type bandage and handed it to Frank. "Here," he said. "That ought to stop the bleeding on his head—at least for now."

Frank carefully applied the pad, with its self-adhesive, to Jeremy's head wound, and it stopped the blood that was still dripping down the side of his face.

"I'll run and get those reflectors," Kip said, and took off, leaving Frank, Joe, and the unconscious Jeremy in the silence of the desolate spot. Within a few minutes Joe started pacing and squinting into the distance. "What's taking them so long?" he said.

"It's probably only been fifteen minutes," Frank said. "It just seems like longer."

A few minutes later, Frank turned to see Kip jogging toward them, carrying the stove heat reflectors. "You were quick," Joe said.

Kip nodded, catching his breath. "I know a shortcut," he said. "We took the slow way out, through all those little canyons. But you can cut right through the biggest one," he said, pointing to a large rock just south of them.

One by one, Kip placed the reflectors on the rocks that surrounded the clearing. As the sun caught them, they sent bright flashes of light into the sky.

Frank, Joe, and Kip waited.

As Kip and Frank scanned the sky all around,

Joe stared at the tops of the canyons where he had been chasing Jorge. He shuffled his feet in the gritty sand, anxious to be on the move.

Finally Joe turned to Frank and Kip. "Look, I can't just stay here. I know this kid didn't go far. I mean, he and Jeremy got lost before. I'm not sure he knows where he's going." He glanced back at the injured teen, lying in Frank's shadow. "Why don't I go after Jorge again while we wait?"

Frank frowned. "What if they come while you're gone?"

"You can take the truck back," Kip offered. "Frank and I can get a ride with the BLM, and you can meet us at the hospital in Moab. Think you can find your way back?"

Joe nodded slowly. "Sure." He looked at Frank. "And maybe I can sort out what happened between these kids."

Frank nodded his agreement, and Kip tossed Joe the keys to the four-wheel-drive truck. Joe threaded his arms through his backpack straps and put the keys in a pocket.

"Don't forget about the shortcut," Kip said.

"Got it," Joe said, and with a quick salute took off for the canyons again.

The sound of Joe's footsteps faded into the distance, and Frank and Kip were again alone in the desert silence. Frank bent over and checked

Jeremy's pulse again. It was faint, but it was still there.

"You're sure they can find us?" Frank asked after a few minutes.

"They should know this area better than I do," Kip said. "But it can take a few minutes to get a chopper staffed and running."

Just as the words were out of Kip's mouth, Frank heard a whirring in the distance. He jerked his head around and saw a small dot in the sky coming toward them. The whirring got closer, and soon the medical rescue helicopter was hovering directly above them, stirring up dust and gravel.

It took only a few moments for the pilot to maneuver the chopper to a landing. With its blades kicking up so much wind and dust, Frank barely noticed a BLM Jeep tearing across the clearing.

The pilot kept the helicopter idling as an emergency technician opened the door and stepped to the ground in a crouch. He was a tall, pudgy man with a buzz cut, wearing a white and orange uniform with an EMT patch on the shoulder. He ran over and nodded at Frank and Kip, then bent over Jeremy, checking the teen's head wound and body bruises. "What happened?" he yelled over the *whop-whop* of the chopper blades.

Frank shook his head. "We don't know. We

found him like this. Looks like he was attacked and beaten up pretty badly."

The technician nodded. "Let's put him inside." He went back to the helicopter and grabbed a stretcher. Frank and Kip helped the EMT lift Jeremy onto it and carry him into the helicopter, where the stretcher fit neatly into a special rack.

The technician bent over Jeremy. "Any idea who he is?" he asked Frank and Kip.

They both shook their heads. "All we know is his name's Jeremy," Frank said.

As the technician grabbed a blood pressure kit, he nodded. "We'll take him to the hospital in Moab," he yelled.

Frank and Kip backed away from the helicopter, bumping into two BLM workers as they did. None of them said anything until the helicopter noisily lifted off again, moving straight up, then banking and heading northeast toward Moab.

"Are you the ones that called?" one of the BLM officials, a short, dark-haired woman, asked.

Kip nodded. He introduced himself and Frank to the man and woman and explained how they had come across Jeremy and Jorge.

The other official, a middle-aged man, said, "Are you sure the other one had water when he took off?"

Frank nodded. "Positive. We saw him grab a water bottle."

The man shrugged. "We haven't had any reports of anyone being lost out here or of groups that got split up. Let's hope this Jeremy can be stabilized. Then he can tell us exactly what happened."

The BLM workers offered Frank and Kip a ride to the Moab hospital with them. They quickly gathered their supplies into their packs again, and before long they were sitting in the back of the Jeep headed for town.

It was a bumpy ride, but it took less than an hour to make it back to Moab. As soon as they reached the hospital, Frank and Kip, along with the rangers, hurried to the emergency room.

There was a short line in front of the admitting desk, and several people sat in the waiting area. But Frank didn't see any sign of Jeremy or a doctor.

Looking down the hallway to the right of the admitting desk, Frank noticed a couple of nurses running into a room. Behind them was the emergency technician who had put Jeremy in the helicopter.

Frank hurried down the hallway with Kip close behind. The technician looked up. "Hey, you aren't supposed to be in this area," he said.

"We just wondered how Jeremy's doing," Frank said.

The technician nodded his head in the direction of the room in front of him. Frank could see through the open door that a few attendants were surrounding an examining table. "He's in there," the technician said. "He was pretty bad. I don't know if they can—"

"Get the electricity!" Somebody shouted from inside the room. "He's flatlining."

Chapter

5

A YOUNG DOCTOR DASHED UP as a nurse handed him electric shock pads, which he slapped onto Jeremy's bare chest.

"Now!" he said. Frank could see Jeremy's feet flop up off the table as the electrical current pulsed through his body. The doctor gave Jeremy three more quick jolts, then with an eye on the heart monitor, he took his pulse again. Several tense seconds later, he nodded to the rest of the emergency team. "Okay, we got it back," he said.

Frank felt a hand on his shoulder and turned to see the emergency technician from the helicopter. "You're going to have to go," the man said. "Only medical personnel are allowed here."

Frank nodded, reluctantly turning to walk

down the hallway. After helping with Jeremy's rescue, Frank felt somewhat responsible for him. Was the battered boy finally out of danger? As Frank and Kip headed for the waiting room, a nurse from the trauma team brushed past them. Frank reached out and touched her arm. "How's that patient?"

The nurse barely looked at him. "His heart's going, but he's still critical," she said, hurrying down the hall. "Too soon to tell if he's going to make it."

Frank and Kip silently moved toward seats in the waiting room. Just as they were about to sit down, though, the doctor from the trauma room appeared in front of them with a police officer next to him.

"Were you the ones who brought the young man in to the emergency room?" the doctor asked.

Both Frank and Kip stood up. "Yes," Frank said. "Well, we called the Bureau of Land Management, and they brought him here."

"I'm Officer Gonzalez," the policeman said. He was tall, with a Moab P.D. patch on his shoulder. "Do you know who he is?"

"He said his name is Jeremy," Frank answered. Then he introduced himself and Kip and explained how they had met Jeremy and Jorge the night before and then again that morning. "All we know is what the two of them said last night," Frank added.

"Did you notice if Jeremy was hurt last night?" the doctor asked.

Frank shook his head. "He was pretty run-down, but he wasn't bruised or bleeding or anything."

"What were the two of them doing in the park without supplies anyway?" the police officer asked.

"We wondered about that ourselves," Kip said. "I thought they might be part of that wilderness survival program. You know . . ."

"You mean Right Directions," Officer Gonzalez said, nodding slowly. Tucking his pen into his spiral notebook, he thanked Frank and Kip. "I'm going to check out the Right Directions roster," he added as he turned to leave.

"How's Jeremy?" Frank asked as the doctor turned to head back to the trauma room.

"Looks like a skull fracture and some deep chest contusions," the doctor said. "He's on a respirator now. Barring complications, there's a better than fifty–fifty chance he'll make a full recovery. But it's going to take time, and he's going to be in a lot of pain. Now, if you'll excuse me, I need to get back to work."

Frank turned to Kip. "So, what else do you know about Right Directions?"

"The director is a guy named Freddy Malin,"

Kip said. "He's been investigated several times by the police. Some people blame the Right Directions kids for any graffiti and vandalism in the park."

"Do they do it?" Frank asked.

Kip shrugged. "I don't think the cops have ever been able to prove anything either way. But some of those kids must be pretty hard cases—almost impossible to control."

"How's the patient?" a voice asked from behind them. Frank turned to see Joe, tired and sweaty, stride into the waiting room.

"Critical," Frank said. "Skull fracture and chest contusions."

"Did you find Jorge?" Kip asked.

Joe sighed and shook his head. "I feel like I've been in and out of every little canyon and up and down every rock in that park. But I couldn't find a trace of him."

"Believe it or not, you probably only scratched the surface," Kip said. "You'd be surprised. There're so many nooks and crannies that you could have been right next to him and not even known it."

Joe rubbed his eyes, which had dark circles of fatigue and dirt smudged under them. "Don't tell me that," he said. "I did find a knapsack though. I left it in the truck. I wonder what the story *is* with those two."

"We were sitting here wondering the same thing," Frank said.

Joe looked around the waiting area. "Can we get something to eat?"

"Yeah," Kip said. "Let's go try the cafeteria." The three followed the signs through a maze of hallways to a well-stocked deli and buffet, half filled with hospital employees and visitors. After lunch the three of them headed back to the admitting desk. The receptionist reported that Jeremy had been moved to the intensive care unit.

Frank led the way up the stairs to ICU. The hallway was quiet except for the occasional *ding* of an elevator door and some low conversation at the nurses' station. As they moved closer to the swinging double doors of the ICU—off limits to the public—they heard a couple of voices raised in anger.

"Look, I'm just tired of getting calls about you people," the deeper voice said. Frank recognized it as belonging to Officer Gonzalez.

"You can get all the calls in the world," a higher, more frantic voice said. "I thought the police were supposed to look for facts. If you'd bother doing that, you'd see there's nothing to worry about."

Frank walked up to a short, frizzy-haired man standing next to the police officer. The shorter man whirled around, his eyes focusing on Kip.

"Well, well, if it isn't the young Mr. Coles,"

the man said. "Fancy meeting you here. Were you the ones who helped out those two trouble-makers?"

Kip, who stood almost a foot taller than the man, answered coolly, "So Jeremy and Jorge were with your program? Freddy Malin, I'd like you to meet my friends Frank and Joe Hardy. Frank and Joe, this is Freddy Malin of Right Directions."

Frank stuck out a hand, but Malin was still glaring at Kip. "So what happened? You hide Jeremy and Jorge safe and sound, then you call in the cavalry just to ruin my reputation? Just wait till you hear about those two. You'll be sorry you ever got mixed up with them. They're nothing but trouble."

Frank frowned at Malin. "What are you talking about?" he said. "We found Jeremy unconscious this morning. Assaulted and battered. We had no idea he was in your program."

"You're lucky someone did find him," Officer Gonzalez said. "He's your responsibility, and if it hadn't been for these boys, he'd probably be dead."

Malin stopped for a beat. "So, where was he?" he said, his voice calmer.

Kip quickly explained their two encounters with Jeremy and Jorge. As he did, Malin shuffled on the hallway carpet, glancing nervously at the doors to the intensive care unit.

When Kip finished, Malin said, "Look, you can't blame Right Directions for what happened to those two. They've been causing trouble ever since they started the program. They picked fights with everyone in the group, including each other. They've just been a pain—I mean, I certainly hope they're going to be okay obviously, but . . ." Malin's voice trailed off.

Frank glanced at Joe. The director was obviously much more concerned about the reputation of his program than about the well-being of the two teens. "If they were in so much trouble, what were they doing out there all by themselves, unsupervised?" Frank asked.

"It's a technique we use all the time for uncontrollable kids," Malin said with a shrug. "We map out a short side trip for just the two of them. They're forced to rely on each other and build some trust and teamwork skills. All these two did was complain, talk back, and refuse to do any work—they were a nightmare."

"I guess it failed then," Joe said. "The teamwork part, that is."

Malin shook his head. "We did what we could. Those two had their chances, but they just wouldn't cooperate. They have a major attitude problem," he said earnestly. "They're definitely what I'd call hard cases."

Frank leveled a gaze at Freddy Malin. An attitude problem? Frank thought back to their night-time encounter with Jeremy and Jorge. The two had been hungry, frightened, and in trouble—and had lied to the Hardys and Kip—but they hadn't seemed particularly dangerous or even especially rude.

The police officer sighed. "Well, the two of them are in trouble now. The one out there wandering around the canyons is wanted for questioning for assault, and the other's going to be in *there* for some time," he said, nodding toward the ICU.

"I know, I know." Malin rubbed his forehead. "That's why I've got about twenty-five phone calls to make. Excuse me, gentlemen." He pulled a cellular phone from his jacket pocket and moved to a seat in the waiting area, punching in a number.

The police officer followed him. "I have to radio in myself," he said.

Frank turned to Kip. "Would you mind postponing the camping trip for a while? I'd like to find out more about Mr. Malin's program and his two 'troublemakers.'"

Kip smiled. "Fine with me. In fact, I think we've got some information on the program back at my uncle's office—just some newspaper clippings and brochures."

"That's a start," Joe said.

The three left the hospital and climbed back into Kip's four-wheeler. Frank picked up a knapsack from the passenger seat. "Is this the one you found?" he asked Joe.

Joe nodded. "I found the remains of a campfire not far from where we found Jeremy, and this was sitting next to it. I figured it was Jorge's, and he didn't have time to grab it when we surprised him. I think it's empty."

Frank turned the dusty, soiled pack over in his hands. Then he checked the front zipper compartment. "Empty except for this," Frank said as he pulled out a crumpled notebook, which looked as if it had gotten wet, then dried out and stiffened. He looked at Kip and Joe. "It says it belongs to Jorge Robles."

Frank finally opened the small, spiral-bound book, peering at the pages while Kip and Joe looked on in silence. He read to himself for a few moments, then looked up, his eyes wide.

"What does it say?" Joe said.

Frank blinked a few times and then started reading. " 'I can't take this. It's crazy. I don't have any food or fresh water. I'm so dizzy I can barely write. I tried to stop and rest yesterday, but they wouldn't let me. I had to keep up with the group even after I threw up.' "

"Sounds pretty rough," Joe said.

Frank nodded. "It must be his diary." Frank flipped to another page and read some more. " 'As bad as I feel, I don't know what to do about Jeremy. There's something wrong with him. He's got all this white stuff around his mouth, like he's foaming or something. And he keeps falling down when he walks. He's all beat up by the rocks and stuff. I told our supervisor, Steve, that Jeremy needs a doctor, but Steve just said that Jeremy's got to toughen up. Yeah, right. Steve's not so tough.' "

Joe let out a breath. "What is this? Some kind of starvation march?" he asked.

"Just about," Frank said, scanning some more pages. "Some of this is pretty desperate sounding. The kids can't get water when they need it, and when they ask for help to take care of blisters or cuts, the supervisors tell them they're acting like babies. According to Jorge anyway."

"He's not the first one," Kip said. "Some other kids have said similar stuff, but Malin's always been able to worm out of any trouble because, so far, all the kids have survived the program and gone on with their lives."

Frank shook his head grimly. "Let's hope Jeremy's not the first fatality."

Joe and Kip nodded silently, and Kip started his truck, heading back to his uncle's office. Frank continued to skim Jorge's penciled scrawlings, passing the notebook to Joe occasionally. Frank's mind was racing. Jorge was out roaming the desert canyon lands alone, Jeremy was in critical condition in the hospital, and Malin was covering up the brutal conditions in his program.

The question Frank had to ask was how far any of them would go to cover up any crimes they'd committed?

Kip pulled the truck into a parking space on the main street just a few buildings up from ExploreUtah. Frank and Joe got out and followed Kip.

Just as Kip was about to put his key in the lock of the glass door, he stopped. Frank looked over his friend's shoulder. The heavy door was partially open.

"Hey," Joe said behind Frank. "I thought your uncle was out on a trip—"

"He is," Kip said under his breath. "And I'm the only other person with a key."

Kip stepped up to the doorway. "Careful," Frank muttered right behind him. As Frank stepped through the half-opened door, trying not to touch anything, he quickly scanned the room. Everything seemed to be in place.

"Uh-oh," Kip said, a step ahead of Frank.

Frank followed Kip's gaze to an open door behind the desk where Ted Coles had sat the previous day. The lock looked as if it had been bashed in.

"It's the equipment storage room," Kip said, moving around his uncle's desk.

Frank and Joe were right behind Kip. It occurred to Frank they might be about to interrupt an intruder. They stepped through the doorway and found the small, windowless room empty. Boxes of clothing, books, climbing ropes, rafting gear, and maps were overturned, and papers were strewn all over the floor.

Kip went straight to a small cabinet in the back of the room. One of its two doors hung open, and the padlock was smashed. Kip peered inside, then turned to Frank and Joe, his face pale.

"Something missing?" Joe said.

"Definitely," Kip said, glancing around the room. "Some maps and equipment, but I'm not worried about them. I'm worried about the gun— Uncle Ted's high-powered hunting rifle. It's gone, and so are the three boxes of ammo that were with it."

Chapter
6

Kip slammed his hand against the gun cabinet, which started its door swinging wildly.

"What is with people in this town?" he yelled. "It used to be you could leave your doors unlocked and not worry about getting ripped off. *Now* look what it's come to!"

"Easy," Joe said. "Let's just keep our cool, see what's missing, clean up the mess, and figure out who could have done this." Joe picked up a box and started to put the contents back inside.

Kip sighed. "Sorry, Joe. You're right. It's just that it was my uncle's special hunting rifle—a beautiful piece with a telescopic sight. He's had it for years." Kip picked up a couple of maps that had been unfolded and thrown aside. "I'll start making a list of everything I notice that's missing."

Frank had begun his own careful search of the cramped storage room, looking for any possible clues. "Has anything like this happened before?" Frank asked.

Kip shook his head. "We've never actually had anyone break in if that's what you mean. But you heard Russ Hyrum. It wouldn't surprise me if he and his buddies decided to step up their game a little."

"But why would Hyrum take a rifle?" Joe asked. "I mean, I could see him wanting to vandalize the business. What would he do with a gun and a few maps? I'm sure he's got plenty of his own."

"Or a canteen?" Kip added, noting another item on his missing inventory list. He shrugged. "I don't know. It doesn't make sense. But Hyrum's never acted logically."

"Seems to me like somebody's going on a camping trip—or a hunting trip—way up in the mountains," Joe said. "Maybe somebody who's on the run."

"Like Jorge?" Frank said. "He'd have to be a lot tougher than he seemed to be in his diary to pull off something like this."

"That diary could be a setup for all we know," Joe said. "And what about Malin? He really seemed to have it in for you and your uncle, Kip."

"He's definitely on the defensive," Kip said. "But how far would he go? I still think we've got to keep an eye on Hyrum.

"Come to think of it," Kip continued, "if Hyrum were going to vandalize any business, it would probably be Right Directions. The only group he hates more than ours is Malin's. He wrote to the local newspaper about them. Called them 'wild packs of dogs let loose on our ancestral lands . . . a criminal element plopped right into our midst.'"

Joe nodded. "Well, it's probably a good idea to talk to Mr. Hyrum. One way or another, he doesn't sound like the kind of guy your uncle would want running around with a high-powered rifle."

"Should we check for fingerprints?" Kip wanted to know.

"It wouldn't really help. There are too many people in and out of here," Frank explained.

The three quickly made it through the litter of maps, storage bags, sleeping bags, ropes, water bottles, and dried food, putting everything back as they wrote a list of all the missing items. Whoever had broken in had probably been in a hurry, since only a couple of local maps, a little food, and the rifle were gone. Kip shut the gun cabinet as best he could and made a note to replace the lock as well as the one on the storage room. Kip made a quick call to report the break-in to the police before they left.

At Kip's suggestion, the three grabbed a burger at a downtown grill and then headed to Uncle Ted's small wooden frame house to spend the night. Though Kip tried to maintain his easy-going manner as he showed the Hardys to a guest bedroom, Frank could tell his friend was rattled by the burglary.

They had all but forgotten their original hiking-and-camping plan, the strange situation of Jeremy and Jorge occupying their full attention now. As Frank felt the cool night air circulate in the house, he wondered if it was this pleasant where Jorge was spending the night.

The next morning there were just a few high, wispy clouds to break up the pure blue expanse of sky as Frank, Joe, and Kip got an early start. Joe called ahead to the hospital and found out that Jeremy had a one-hour visiting period that morning.

"You're probably so used to this kind of weather, you take it for granted," Joe remarked to Kip as he gazed out through the windshield.

A smile spread across Kip's face for the first time that morning. "Nope," he said. "That big blue sky is just as amazing now as it was when I was a kid."

At the hospital they hurried past the big curved reception desk. Joe led the way up the stairs, taking them in his usual style—two at a time.

"They said his room is just two doors to the right of the stairs," he called back to Kip and Frank. Joe swung open the metal door, but just as he stepped into the carpeted hallway, somebody burst past, bumping Joe's shoulder as he went toward the stairwell.

"Hey, slow down," Joe said. He turned around to see the figure dash past Frank and Kip and fly down the stairs. The person had a baseball cap pulled down low and a lightweight tan parka worn over jeans. Joe thought it looked like a man, but he couldn't even be sure of that.

"That guy was in too much of a hurry," Joe said.

"I guess hospitals make some people really nervous," Kip commented as they continued down the hallway.

Suddenly a sharp, repetitive buzz, like the noise of an alarm clock, sounded. Frank and Joe raced to the second door on the right. Jeremy's frail body lay on a bed. Next to the bed, the alarm was sounding on a large respirator.

Joe ran over to the machine. "He's dead!" he cried. Frank quickly strode to the side of the bed and grabbed Jeremy's wrist. This time he couldn't feel a pulse.

"I'll get a doctor," Kip said, taking off down

the hall. Joe sprinted out of the room after Kip, dashing to the stairway exit to see if he could catch whoever had been in such a hurry to leave.

Meanwhile Frank pulled off Jeremy's bedcovers and positioned the heel of one hand on the teen's chest. Putting his right hand on top of his left, he began CPR, rhythmically counting the short pumps to his heart.

Seconds later Kip, two nurses, and a doctor appeared next to Frank. The doctor, a tall, middle-aged woman, nodded at Frank and immediately took over the resuscitation efforts. One of the nurses flicked a couple of switches on the respirator, then bent down to peer under it.

Frank watched as the nurse grabbed an electrical cord and plugged it into the outlet on the wall. "Somebody unplugged this thing," she said, getting to her feet and scowling at Frank.

The hum and steady beep of the respirator filled the room again. In another minute the doctor held her stethoscope to Jeremy's chest. "Okay, he's breathing," she said, her face flushed from her exertion. She turned to Frank and Kip. "Now, what happened here?"

Joe suddenly ran into the room, panting. "Whoever it was is gone," he said. "I didn't see anyone in the stairwell or the parking lot."

"Whoever *who* was?" the doctor said. "Do you know who unplugged this machine?"

Joe shook his head. "Nope. All I know is we

saw someone leaving the floor in a big hurry just as we got here. Then we heard this alarm go off."

The nurse who had plugged in the respirator was still scowling at the three boys. "So, we're supposed to take your word for this?"

Frank's eyes flicked up at her. "Why would we want to hurt him?" he said. "We're the ones who brought him in. You saw me—I was doing CPR on him when you walked in."

"And if we did want to hurt him, why would we stick around to talk to you?" Joe added.

The nurse nodded slowly. "Anyway, I'm calling the police," she said, leaving the room.

Frank was lost in thought, his eyes fixed on Jeremy's pasty face. Somebody wanted to kill him pretty badly to come into the hospital and unplug his respirator. It was the second time in twenty-four hours they had found Jeremy nearly dead. There had to be more to it than just a fight between him and his camping buddy, Jorge.

"Is he going to be all right?" Joe asked.

The doctor watched the numbers on the respirator intently. "His condition is still critical," she said. "But he's breathing again—with help. The next twenty-four hours will be crucial to see how the skull fracture heals. He's quite fragile at this point."

"Are any of you family members?" the nurse asked.

Again Frank shook his head. "Right now," he said, "we don't even know his last name."

The doctor picked up the chart at the end of Jeremy's bed. "Reis," she said.

A brief silence fell on the room. Frank nodded and thanked the doctor, and after another brief glance at Jeremy Reis, the three left the room.

As Frank, Joe, and Kip made their way down to the main floor, Kip was the first to speak. "This is way out of hand," he said quietly. "What's up with this kid that somebody would want to kill him this badly?"

Frank could only shake his head. "Did you get any kind of look at the person running down the stairs?" he asked Joe.

"Not really," Joe said. "I'd say he was about five-foot-eight, medium build. Seems like he had a quick escape route planned."

"Do you think it was Jorge?" Kip asked. "Do you think it was just that they had a fight?"

"Could be," Frank said. "But they were both in the same boat, wandering around the canyons. Even if they did have a tussle, what would make Jorge angry enough to come back and kill Jeremy? We've got to find Jorge and/or dig up some evidence."

They had arrived at the guard's station on the first floor, and Frank approached the young officer on duty, Officer Jack Krieger. It turned out he was the older brother of one of Kip's high school classmates. After introducing the Hardys, Kip explained what had just happened in Jeremy's room. Then Frank and Joe filled the officer in on the rest of the case.

"We'd like to find out what's going on with the two of them," Frank said. "We feel sort of responsible for them."

"Frank and Joe have a lot of investigative experience, Jack," Kip explained to Officer Krieger. "Their dad's a top PI back East. Maybe if we help you guys out, you could help us."

The officer had listened in silence to the story, but now he frowned. "First of all, Kip, you know I can't extend any official cooperation to amateur detectives, but of course, I'll see what I can do unofficially. Second, it sounds like it's Officer Gonzalez's investigation. And third, normally I'd say we're going to be all over it. It sounds like there's definitely something up with that wilderness program. But we just got called in to assist the Colorado State Police on a manhunt. There's a prisoner by the name of"—he flipped through his notes—"John Bryson, who just escaped from a maximum security state facility up there. They're saying there's a good chance he crossed the border and is headed this way. He's being considered armed and extremely dangerous. They're pulling in every spare cop."

Frank and Joe looked at each other. If they

were going to help Jeremy, it looked as if they would be doing it on their own.

"I'll go up and take another look around the intensive care unit," the officer said. "And I'll increase my rounds up there, too. You fellows let us know if you come across anything, okay?"

Frank and Joe agreed and thanked him, and the three of them went back outside to Kip's truck.

"Now what?" Kip asked.

"We need some background on Jeremy and Jorge," Joe said.

Frank turned to Kip. "Do you know where the Right Directions office is?"

Kip nodded. "Not far from here—nothing is far from anything in Moab."

"Let's pay a visit," Joe said.

Within minutes, Kip had pulled into a quiet side street just a few blocks from the ExploreUtah offices. He parked in front of a one-story brick house on a corner. A small wooden sign pounded into the lawn in front had the words Right Directions carved into it.

"I'm not so sure we'll get a warm reception," Frank said, "so maybe one of us should stay in the car in case Joe stirs up his usual amount of trouble and we need to make a quick getaway." He winked at his brother.

"I'll wait," Kip volunteered. "I'll park right down the street and keep the engine running."

Frank got out and led the way up the short front walk. "The direct approach?" Joe asked.

"You have a better way?" Frank replied.

With a shake of his head, Joe followed Frank up a couple of cement steps. Frank put his hand to the door, knocking a couple of times.

The door swung open, but there was no one inside.

"Hello?" Frank called. He stepped into the doorway. "Hello?" he tried again.

There was no answer. Frank looked around. There was a small room on each side of the entryway. One was set up as a reception area, with shelves displaying brochures and information packets, a small television, and an oversize couch. The other room had a desk, a couple of file cabinets, and a round table covered with papers.

Frank took a few steps farther into the house, Joe right behind him.

"Anybody home?" Joe called out. When no one answered, Joe moved quickly down the hall to the back of the house. "Looks like a storage room and office space and a little kitchen," he called back to Frank.

Joe came back to the front of the house, where Frank was poking through the Right Directions brochures in the reception area. "Strange," Joe said, "The door's open, but no one's here."

"Remember what Kip said about people being able to leave their doors unlocked?" Frank said, glancing out the front window. "Maybe they still practice that custom here at Right Directions. Now let's see if we can take advantage of it and dig up some info on Jorge and Jeremy."

After one more check of the back of the house, Joe moved over to the office area. He slid open the top drawer of one filing cabinet while Frank opened the other. For a couple of minutes, as Frank and Joe went through files, the only sound in the small room was the ticking of a wall clock.

Frank couldn't see much method to the system of the files. Some had the names of people on them, whereas others had years or places written on them. "This could take forever," he muttered.

"No kidding," Joe said. "There's stuff in here that doesn't have anything to do with the business—"

"Wait a minute," Frank said suddenly. He pulled open a thin manila file folder. " 'Robles, Jorge. Reis, Jeremy,' " he read. His eyes scanned down a few lines. Then he looked up at Joe.

"Jeremy and Jorge were sent to this program after they were involved in a couple of armed robberies," he said, his voice echoing in the quiet room. "They testified against a third partner and got off easy."

A car horn sounded two quick beeps outside.

Frank looked up. "That's Kip," he said in a hoarse whisper. Just then they heard footsteps coming up the walkway. "Somebody's coming."

Chapter

7

FRANK AND JOE both snapped to attention.

Frank tucked the file under his arm and carefully shut the drawer with his elbow. Joe clicked the drawers shut on the cabinet he had been going through, took a quick glance around the small room, and grabbed Frank's elbow, pulling him through a darkened doorway in the corner.

It was a tiny bathroom; Joe positioned the door so that it was open just a crack. Frank had backed up as far as the toilet when he heard the front door opening. The Hardys peered through the crack, Joe crouching down and Frank leaning over him. They couldn't see much, but they could hear someone creeping in.

The light clicked on, and there was a rolling

sound followed by some rustling. Someone else was doing exactly what they had been doing a few minutes earlier—snooping through the files. Who was it? Frank wondered.

Frank shifted, being careful not to bump into Joe. His leg banged into the toilet, bending his knee at an awkward angle. Trying to get his balance, he swung his arm out, smacked the medicine cabinet, and sent the contents clattering down, shattering the silence in the little office. Frank heard Joe groan as the intruder slammed the file drawer and took off, bumping into a chair and knocking it over as he fled.

"He's bolting," Joe hissed, throwing the bathroom door open. As he stepped into the office, he glimpsed the back of a slim, dark-haired man stuffing a manila folder under his shirt and running for the door.

Joe charged out the front door and leaped down the front steps with Frank on his heels. They caught sight of the dark-haired figure running around to the back of the house. Frank turned and saw Kip running up the front lawn, pointing toward the intruder. "That way," Kip yelled.

Joe ran around the side of the house and turned right into the alley, then pulled up short.

The intruder, about twenty yards down the alley, had spun around and was facing them. They found themselves staring at Jorge Robles.

"Jorge," Joe called out, advancing slowly. "Wait! We're trying to help you."

But the teen, a look of utter panic on his face, turned and sprinted down the alley.

Joe raced toward Jorge, his eyes trained on the back of the teen's torn T-shirt. He could hear Frank and Kip close behind him.

Suddenly Jorge darted into an opening on his left and disappeared somewhere in a row of houses that backed up to the alleyway. Joe ran to where he thought Jorge had turned, a small passageway between the backyards of two houses. But it was empty.

Joe turned to Frank and Kip. Panting, he said, "It was Jorge. Did you see him?" As the two nodded, he pointed down the alley and said to Kip, "Keep going this way. Frank, when we come out onto the street, I'll go right, and you go left." Without a word, Frank followed Joe down the narrow strip of cement between the two houses.

Joe ran out onto the street, his eyes darting around for any glimpse of Jorge. He went right, slipping behind parked cars and around hedges. He looked over his shoulder and saw Frank doing the same thing down the block.

Joe had seen the look of desperation in Jorge's eyes: He was running scared. Maybe he'd sneaked into a house or garage.

Joe ran to where the block intersected a wider and busier street. There were several passersby but no Jorge. Joe turned and ran back down the street toward Frank, spending the next few minutes dashing in and out of every opening between houses, but it was futile. The kid had disappeared again.

Joe met up with Frank near where they had started. "Any sign of him?" Frank asked.

"Nope," Joe said. "He's good at that, like some kind of escape artist. That's the second time he's slipped by me—no problem."

Frank and Joe ducked between the two houses and came out onto the alley, waving to Kip, who was still searching at the far end.

Frank shrugged. "He obviously wanted something because he took a file with him. I just wish we could talk to him, give him a chance to explain."

He turned as Kip caught up to them, and the three began walking to the end of the alley.

"Whatever it is," Frank continued, "I hope we get some answers from these files," he said, tapping the front of his shirt, where he had stuffed Jeremy's and Jorge's files. He turned to Kip. "Turns out Jeremy and Jorge were in the Right Directions program because they got nailed for a couple of armed robberies."

Kip whistled softly as they came out of the alley. "So maybe . . ."

Joe grabbed his arm and turned around suddenly. "Did you hear that?" Joe said.

"Hear what?" Kip asked.

Joe shook his head and lowered his voice. "I think somebody's following us."

"I thought that's what *we* were supposed to be doing," Kip said.

Frank turned and checked back down the alley. "Did you see anybody?" he asked Joe.

Joe frowned. "I don't know. I thought I heard somebody but maybe not."

With Frank still looking around, the three slowly walked back to Kip's truck. As Kip pulled the driver's door open, he stopped suddenly. He stared at the driver's seat for a few seconds and then looked away in disgust. "Oh, please," he said finally.

Frank pulled open the passenger door. "What is it?" he asked.

Kip picked up a piece of white lined paper that had obviously been torn from a notebook and handed it to Frank. "Looks like another of Hyrum's stupid games," he said.

Frank looked at the message on the paper: "Stay out of my way. Otherwise someone gets hurt." Frank turned the sheet over to check the back of it, which was blank. He handed it to Joe, who quickly read it.

"How do you know it was Hyrum?" Frank asked.

"Tell me that doesn't sound like something Hyrum would say," Kip said.

Frank shrugged. "Sounds to me like almost anyone could have said it." He looked across the street at the Right Directions building and then up and down the block. "And somebody didn't have much time. You weren't out of the car that long."

"Jorge?" Joe asked.

"Maybe," Frank said. "Once he gave us the slip, he could have made it back here for a few seconds."

"I doubt he'd have the presence of mind," Kip said.

"How about Freddy Malin?" Frank said. "It's his property. Maybe he spotted us searching the neighborhood."

"Could be," Kip said. "I'm just used to Hyrum's antics so I automatically blame him."

"Let's hold on to that," Frank said, taking the sheet back from Joe.

"As detectives, maybe you two can figure out who wrote it," Kip said. "Since we lost Jorge, it won't matter if we stop and have a quick lunch. That way you can do your detecting on a full stomach."

The three climbed into the truck, and within a few minutes, Kip had pulled in front of what looked like a renovated warehouse. "Best burgers in town," he said. "Guaranteed."

The three were seated in the back of a large, lofty room with exposed steel beams and track lighting. After a young, blond waitress took their orders, Frank pulled out the two files he had been carrying. He took in the other customers, who appeared to be college students, before opening them.

As he scanned through Jeremy's and Jorge's personal files, Frank murmured, "So the two of them joined the program at the same time. It looks like the judge in their case didn't want them to serve prison time since they were only accomplices to the robberies. The judge said she believed the two were basically taking orders from—"

Suddenly Frank stopped, his face slack. He raised his eyes slowly. "The leader of their gang was John Bryson—"

"The convict who just escaped from prison in Colorado," Joe said.

Chapter

8

KIP SAT BACK in his chair. "No wonder Jorge's running scared. He may have an escaped con bent on revenge following him."

"He may not even know Bryson escaped," Joe said.

"I'd say there's a pretty good chance he does," Frank said, still scanning the folders in front of him. "The way he's been sneaking around, I wouldn't be surprised if he's been at the hospital, and he may have even seen Bryson."

"So, you think Bryson was the one who attacked Jeremy?" Joe asked.

"It's a good possibility," Frank said. "But we don't have any proof that he even knows about Jeremy and Jorge being in Right Directions," he added.

The three were silent for a moment while the waitress set their plates in front of them. Frank kept reading the files, and Joe leaned over to read along. Then Kip spoke up. "You know, if I had just broken out of prison, I'd be keeping a pretty low profile. I don't know that I'd risk showing my face to Jeremy or Jorge or anybody else."

Frank nodded. "The first place the cops would check would be with your former accomplices."

"Good point," Joe said. "But revenge is a pretty strong motive, and we don't know how nuts this Bryson guy is. If he's quick enough and resourceful enough, he could be in and out of here before anybody knew what hit them."

Frank bit into his burger. "So, we keep an eye out for Bryson. Meanwhile, I still want to find out more about Freddy Malin and Right Directions. If Jorge's diary and those other kids' stories are true, then Malin's got a few answers to cough up."

Within fifteen minutes the three of them had wolfed down their lunch and were heading back to the hospital to check on Jeremy. Frank noticed that Joe and Kip were also riding in silence, their eyes checking the streets for any sign of the fugitives.

Minutes later, as they approached Jeremy's room, they heard the unmistakable nasal whine of Freddy Malin's voice. Frank glanced over at

Kip, who rolled his eyes. "Here we go again," Kip muttered.

This time Malin was in the middle of a conversation with Officer Gonzalez and a colleague. "I'm telling you, you should be looking for Jorge Robles in Colorado," Malin was saying. "That's where his family is from. Just outside Pueblo." He lowered his voice slightly. "He doesn't get along with his parents, but they all go home when they run away from the program—back to fighting with their parents and hanging out with their hoodlum friends."

Gonzalez scowled at Malin. "We have absolutely no proof that Robles actually ran away from your program. He could just be lost. And since we've got a pretty good idea that Bryson crossed the state line into Utah, we can't take any chances that he'll find these two boys here."

"Where'd you get that information about Bryson?" Malin blurted out.

"That's privileged information," Gonzalez said. "Now, we expect your full cooperation with this investigation or we'll be forced to—"

"All right, okay, I get your point, Officer," Malin interrupted.

Frank noticed Kip trying to catch his eye. Kip moved closer and whispered, "Do we tell them about Jorge?"

Frank shook his head slightly, trying not to attract the cops' attention. They had no idea where

Jorge had gone, and there was no way Frank was going to explain what he and Joe were doing in Malin's office when they saw Jorge there.

By now Malin and the cops had acknowledged the Hardys' and Kip's presence but were too absorbed in their own conversation to pay much attention to them.

"Look, here's the situation," the other cop said. He was a stocky man with a crew cut whose nameplate read Reusch. "We're focusing our search north and east of the city. We're taking the helicopter up this afternoon so we can cover as much territory as possible. We're assuming you'll be searching to the south and west for Robles. Can we count on it?"

"I told you already," Malin said. "We're conducting our own search. You all can do whatever you want with your helicopter, and you don't need our help to do it. Now, if you don't mind, I'm going to go away and mind my own business."

With that, Malin turned and headed for the elevators. Frank gave a quick nod to Joe, indicating that he and Kip should check on Jeremy. Then Frank walked swiftly down the carpeted hallway, following the Right Directions program director.

"They can head due south for all I care," the frizzy-haired man was muttering to himself.

As Malin stopped at the elevator, jabbing the

Down button angrily, Frank bent over a drinking fountain. Out of the corner of his eye, he could see Malin glaring at the police officers down the hall. "Obviously, he went west," he said under his breath as the elevator doors opened. Stepping inside, he disappeared from view.

Frank stood up. Why was Malin so sure of Jorge's whereabouts? And why didn't he share his hunch with the police? Frank didn't understand the man's anger. It would have made much more sense if Malin were *worried* about Jeremy and Jorge, not to mention the cops' renewed interest in his program. Instead, he was defensive and angry.

Frank walked back to Jeremy's room and met up with Joe and Kip. "The patient's asleep," Joe said. "The nurse said that as long as his vital signs continue to improve, he'll probably be moved out of intensive care tomorrow. But they're still going to watch him closely."

Frank nodded, glancing into Jeremy's room. He looked safe and peaceful as he lay with his eyes closed, surrounded by blinking machines. Frank just hoped the room would stay this quiet.

When they got back to the truck, Frank told Joe and Kip about Malin's mutterings.

"So Malin's going after Jorge," Joe said. "Trying to beat the cops to the punch. Maybe we could beat *him* to it."

"Meanwhile, Jorge risked getting caught to

break into Malin's office and take a file folder," Frank said.

"Maybe he's trying to get some more information on the program so he can nail Malin," Joe said. "Whatever was in that file plus Jorge's diary could be pretty incriminating."

"Malin probably doesn't know what's missing from the files yet, and he may not know about the diary at all," Kip said.

"Maybe," Joe said. "But he'd probably figure Jorge was keeping one. I bet a lot of kids do." Joe turned to Kip suddenly. "Do you think it was Jorge who broke in and took your uncle's rifle and that other stuff?"

"If I thought someone was after me and I was trying to get away cross-country, I guess I'd make sure I had food and maps," Kip said, "and maybe a gun."

"But not unless you were planning on using it against someone," Joe said.

"Possibly," Kip said. "But maybe just for general protection."

They all fell silent, and Kip started up his truck and headed back to downtown Moab. As he did, Frank pulled out Jorge's diary again. He flipped through the pages, with Joe reading over his shoulder from the backseat.

"Sounds like Jorge wasn't too happy to be in Right Directions from the start," Joe commented, breaking the silence, "And he never did like Malin's attitude."

"True," Frank said. "Looks like he was taking an interest in history here. Did you see this part?" Frank flipped back a few pages and read aloud: " 'Now I know why Butch Cassidy would have hidden out around here. No one would want to look for him here. It's too deserted and there's too many places to hide.' "

Frank turned a few more pages and then read, " 'I think the Hole in the Wall Gang actually passed through this same canyon. I guess they thought they could find a better hiding place somewhere else. Makes me wonder about Robbers Roost. This place could probably give it a good run for the money.' "

Kip pulled the truck in front of the ExploreUtah office, barely putting it in park before turning excitedly to the Hardys. "Maybe that's why Malin's convinced that Jorge would head west," he said. "If he had sneaked a peek at Jorge's diary when they were out camping, that could be it. Robbers Roost is west of Canyonlands. Jorge seems to think it's the best place to hide out around these parts. If he's on the run from Malin and from Bryson, I'd be willing to bet that's where he headed.

"There are some pretty rough areas there," Kip said. "You can tell from the names—Dirty

Devil River, No Man's Canyon. You wouldn't want to get lost out there."

"I'd say his going there is a long shot," Frank said.

"Hold on," Joe interrupted. "We know Jorge's on the run from the police or Malin or Bryson. There's a good chance he took those ExploreUtah camping supplies. He's not from around here so he doesn't know too many places to go. I say we go out toward Robbers Roost. If he took off and hitched far from here, we'd have no chance of finding him. But this is a possibility at least, and the *only* lead we have to follow. Besides, if Malin finds him out there, I think we'd better be there, too—then maybe we can unravel this whole mess."

"Joe's got a point," Kip said to Frank. "What do you say?"

"Okay," Frank said, "we might as well start there. We can't do anything else."

Joe was already jumping out of the truck.

"This'll take some careful preparation," Kip said. "We want to have plenty of water and emergency supplies."

The three spent the next half hour adding to their supplies and repacking their backpacks, making sure they had water, water purification tablets, and medical supplies. Kip took a well-worn topographical map and showed Frank and Joe the canyons where they were headed: to the west of Canyonlands National Park. They were near the Henry Mountains. Frank and Joe could see that the terrain was very different from that of Canyonlands with its jagged formations.

Kip drove them out of Moab, heading north around Canyonlands and west to the small town of Hanksville. From there, he turned south and eventually turned left onto a dirt road, which he followed until he came to a quiet river.

Parking the truck, he said, "This is it, guys, the Fremont River. We'll go the rest of the way on foot. It's called the Dirty Devil in these parts. It's pretty shallow, so we'll cross here and then head into No Man's Canyon. This area doesn't get too many visitors—maybe a handful a week. So if anybody's out here, there's a pretty good shot it's someone we're looking for."

"How would Jorge get out here then?" Joe wanted to know.

"Oh, there's some long-distance hauling through here. He'd have no trouble hitching with a trucker," Kip answered.

The landscape had changed a lot. Here, away from the national park, the mesas were much flatter and the formations had much sharper edges, as if they'd been cut by a knife. Frank looked up at the sky; large black clouds were gathering as thunder rumbled in the distance. A few fat raindrops greeted him as he stepped from the truck.

Kip pulled the packs out of the back. "Well, a little afternoon rain never hurt anybody," he said. "Unless it's more than a little," he added quietly, glancing at the big thunderheads rolling in across the mesa.

With their packs in place and the truck locked, the three took off, wading across the shallow Dirty Devil River. Then they hiked across flat rock tops, some of which dropped off suddenly, whereas others stepped down more gradually onto the sandy ground.

Frank could see Joe carefully taking in the area as they walked. He did the same. The rain was coming down harder now, making the path muddy in some places and slippery in others. The vast landscape spread out for miles around them, and Frank was beginning to wonder if they could ever find Jorge here. Even if they were in the right general area, they could walk for miles and never see him.

They trudged on, carefully climbing down around a steep rock into a narrow canyon. The rock rose up on both sides of them in strange swirling shapes, and it echoed the sound of the heavy raindrops. Joe pushed his wet hair from his eyes, and Frank could see the look of impatience on his face. He could tell Joe was just as doubtful as he was about their chances of finding Jorge.

Frank put his head down and plowed ahead.

Then, as they came around a curve where the canyon narrowed, he stopped. There was a small, oblong-shaped piece of metal lying beside the trail about fifteen feet ahead. He went over and picked it up and saw the spring-hinged side. Looking at it even more closely, he noticed *TC* etched by hand into the metal. "Hey, guys," he called out to Kip and Joe, who were ahead of him.

As the two turned around, Frank held up the piece. "A carabiner," Kip said, recognizing the small piece of equipment used to hold climbing ropes.

Frank nodded. "Does your uncle mark his?" he asked Kip.

"Yeah, he scratches his initials in them," Kip said.

Frank showed him the *TC* in the carabiner. Kip's eyes flickered. "That's Uncle Ted's all right," he said. "Good eye, Frank."

"So whoever's been down here may be using the equipment he stole from your office," Joe said.

"This is good," Kip said. "It could mean we're on the right track."

Frank looked straight up to the tops of the rocky bluffs on either side of them. Was there somebody up there watching them? Or waiting to ambush them?

They moved on, climbing out of the canyon.

As they came into a clear, flat area, all three of them looked around. They were outside the shelter of the canyon now, and it seemed to be raining harder. The browns and whites of the landscape merged in the rain.

A few yards ahead, Frank saw Kip bend down. Looking over Kip's shoulder, Frank saw him poking at some wet, smeared ashes on the ground, sending trickles of black sliding across the rock.

"Campfire?" Joe asked.

Kip nodded. "Yep. I wonder who set it. No experienced hiker would start a fire here. They'd know better than that. There's just not enough fuel in this area, so they'd use a camp stove."

"So whoever used this is probably new to the area and maybe new to backpacking," Frank said.

"Which includes our friend Jorge," Joe added.

"All I can say is somebody came through here not long ago and set a campfire," Kip said.

The three stood up, and Joe suddenly yelled, "Hey!"

Frank turned his head to look in the direction Joe was pointing. About a hundred yards ahead, on a slightly higher shelf of the same rock stood Jorge Robles, staring right back at them.

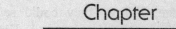

Chapter

9

THEY COULD BARELY MAKE OUT Jorge's face, but it was obvious that just about every muscle in his body was tight with fear. The instant he saw them, he turned and ran down the gentle slope of the rock.

Joe took off after him with Frank and Kip close behind. Within seconds, Frank could feel his legs tighten as he worked hard to keep his balance on the rockface, which was slick with the rainwater. Ahead of him, Joe just kept charging down the slippery rock.

"Careful, guys," Kip yelled from the rear. "Watch for drop-offs."

Sure enough, Jorge's fleeing figure suddenly dropped out of sight, almost as if he had been swallowed up by the sandstone. Joe kept his pace, then hesitated for a moment when he reached the edge. It was about a six-foot drop to the next rock, with a long, narrow crevice in between the two. Joe jumped down, using the full flex of his leg muscles to cushion his landing before taking off again.

"Careful," Kip said to Frank when they reached the edge. Below, they could see Joe sprinting after Jorge, gaining ground. Kip and Frank braced themselves with their hands, and then each took a flying leap. Frank could feel the weight of his pack hit him hard as he landed.

Kip landed with a "Humph." As they took off again, he said, "There're slots and edges like that all over the place. Just watch it."

The two of them raced after Joe, who was stepping gingerly down some declining ledges.

"Hey, Jorge!" Joe yelled out. "We're trying to help you. Hold up. It's Frank and Joe Hardy."

The teen glanced over his shoulder quickly. Then Frank saw his steps slow as he went into a crouch.

"Looks like he's going down some kind of hole," Joe said between breaths as Kip and Frank caught up to him.

The three made their way to a circular opening in the rockface, and Frank peered down into it. About ten feet in diameter, it gradually narrowed toward the bottom, about thirty feet down. Using his hands and feet like a spider's legs, Jorge was inching his way down.

"Jorge!" Joe yelled. "Get out of there!"

"Do I hear water down there?" Frank said, kneeling to lean farther into the hole.

"Yep," Kip said. "When it rains, some of these tributary washes can fill up really fast." He knelt next to Frank. "This one sounds like it's pretty full."

Joe yelled for Jorge to stop again, but he was plunging down the hole, his hands and feet sliding on the slick rock.

"He's going to fall in the water," Joe said between gritted teeth. He yanked off his pack and jumped into the hole, wedging himself with his feet.

"I'm going after him, guys. You get a rope," Joe said, gripping the walls with his fingers splayed. "Jorge, hang on," Joe called. "We'll get you out."

In a flash Kip pulled off his pack, opened it, and took out a climbing rope, harness, and chop blocks. He stepped into the harness and attached the rope. "We'll need a spotter," he said to Frank, who quickly placed the chop blocks in a nearby rock to secure the rope. "Stay here and get the best grip you can on that thing."

Frank nodded, wiping his wet hands on the inside of his shirt, then making sure all the carabiners were fastened as Kip lowered himself into the hole. Frank positioned himself on the edge, watching the three figures below as he checked the rope to make sure it held.

Kip quickly slid down the rope to a ledge beside Joe, who was about ten feet above the water. Just then Jorge finally lost his grip, collapsed, and banged into one side of the hole. Frank heard a faint cry and saw a flash of Jorge's white T-shirt. Jorge's arms flailed around for a grip but caught nothing, and he slid into the rushing stream below.

Joe lunged for Jorge but lost his own grip and slid up to his knees in the churning water as Jorge was washed away. Kip reacted quickly and grabbed Joe by the arm. Frank watched the rope bounce and stretch near the blocks as he braced himself against the brownish red rock.

"The ledge!" Kip yelled. "Grab hold of the ledge I'm on, Joe!"

With his free hand, Joe managed to snag the ledge where Kip was perched. Kip yanked hard, and Joe flopped onto the rock like a big fish on dry land. Joe wriggled up, and struggled to his feet.

Kip and Joe caught their breath, then hauled themselves up to the next ledge, which was larger. Frank kept a steady grip on the anchor above.

Frank heard Joe raise his voice over the roaring of the stream. "Don't you think one of us should go after him?"

Kip shook his head. "Bad idea. Let's just get out of here while we can."

Joe nodded, and the two of them started to work their way back up. It was a struggle, and as soon as they were within arm's length, Frank reached down and hauled each of them up to his level.

The three sat in silence for a moment and caught their breath. Joe and Kip rested their raw hands while the rain continued to fall. Shivering, Joe pulled off his soaked shirt, took a dry one out of his pack, and put it on with a rain jacket over it. Then he turned to Kip and Frank. "We almost had him," he said. He paused and glanced back down the hole. "Do you think he'll make it out of there?"

Kip ran his fingers through his wet hair. "He could," he said, "as long as he doesn't panic."

Frank raised his eyebrows. He knew Jorge had been in a panic well before he fell into the stream, which meant things didn't look good for him. "Where does the stream run?" he asked Kip.

Kip pointed south. "It probably follows this canyon at the bottom of our ledge here. We can get down there if we just keep following this rock."

Joe grabbed his pack. "Let's do it," he said.

Kip and Frank hefted their packs onto their backs again. "Once we get to the bottom," Kip said, "we should think about setting up camp and getting dry. It could rain like this all night." He looked at Frank and Joe intently. "Jorge's in trouble, and we want to help, but we've got to make sure we stay healthy and safe so we can help him."

"Good point," Frank said, and they set off down the rock face. It took several minutes for them to work their way to the bottom, zigzagging to avoid several sheer drop-offs and some broken-up patches of rock. By the time they reached a ledge that ran parallel to the water-filled canyon, the rain had let up a little, and they weren't being constantly pelted anymore.

The three of them walked along the ledge for about three hundred yards as it sloped downward and finally leveled off with the sandy bottom. Frank peered at the sides of the narrow canyon with the water rushing down through it, wondering how Jorge could possibly have found footing on the bottom or pulled himself out. Then he scanned the immediate area. If Jorge did get out, there was no sign of it.

They kept following the stream as it spread out on the sandy floor of the canyon. It got wider and shallower until it had almost petered out about three-quarters of a mile from its narrowest part. All three of them kept a close lookout for any sign of human presence. They had been hiking for about twenty minutes when Joe suddenly pointed to an open space on the other side of the stream. "Hey, what's that?" he asked. "See, over there?"

Frank looked across the water. "What?" he said.

"That plastic thing," Joe said.

"Let's check it out," Kip said, wading into the stream. Joe headed straight for a small, jagged outcropping of rock. He bent down, picked up the object, and held it out for Frank and Kip to see.

"That's one of our water bottles," Kip said. It was a clear plastic bottle with the ExploreUtah logo printed on its side.

"Was that one of the items missing from the storeroom?" Frank asked.

"It was," Kip said. "Uncle Ted had a bunch of those printed as a promotional giveaway."

"Do you think Jorge dropped it?" Frank asked.

"If it was, that means he made it out of that wash," Joe said. "The bottle couldn't have landed all the way down here unless he walked out of there. This water's been barely moving for the last few hundred yards."

"Right," Frank said as he gazed up at the towering rock formations ahead of them.

Kip followed Frank's gaze. "If he did make it out, he's headed east, away from the Dirty Devil, deeper into Robbers Roost Canyon." He turned to Frank. "Maybe those diary entries are pointing us in the right direction after all."

"The only problem is if we don't catch him before he makes it to Robbers Roost," Joe said, "we may never find him. Butch Cassidy and his gang holed up there—because it was practically impossible to find them."

"Well, at least we have a better sense of where he could be than we did this afternoon," Frank said. "We can't lose sight of that."

The rain had completely let up, but the sky was getting dark. Pretty soon it would be impossible to search anymore, so they decided to set up camp for the night. They chose a flat spot not far from the stream. After their dinner, which they ate hungrily, Frank, Joe, and Kip set up their tents again. Before he went to sleep, Frank took a few minutes to stare up at the black shadows of the rocks all around their campsite. Once again he wondered where Jorge would be spending the night.

Despite the bright sunlight streaming through the nylon tent the next morning, Frank took his time waking up, savoring the few moments before he was totally conscious. Just as he yawned and stretched and had a few fuzzy thoughts about drifting back to sleep, he heard a sharp cry cut through the morning silence. "Hey, what's going on here?" It was Kip.

Frank quickly pulled himself from his sleeping bag and saw Joe snap out of his dreams, too. Crawling from the tent, Frank saw Kip standing over his backpack, which was laid open with its contents strewn across the dusty ground.

"It was ransacked," Kip said angrily, his eyes roving around suspiciously.

"Did somebody say ransacked?" Joe mumbled, rubbing his eyes as he emerged from the tent.

"That's right, somebody went through my pack," Kip said, kneeling to sift through its contents.

"Could it have been an animal?" Joe asked.

Kip shook his head firmly. "The food was all put away, and that hasn't even been touched," he said. "That's what an animal would go for. What's missing is our water—and our water purification tablets."

Frank and Joe became silent. Of all the supplies they had, the water was probably the most important. There was no way they could hike through the desert without it.

"Somebody out there knows exactly what they're doing," Joe said grimly.

"Anybody want to bet that that somebody was Jorge?" Kip said.

"Whatever," Frank said. "Right now we need to find water. Got any ideas, Kip?"

Kip was quiet for a moment. Then he squinted up at the rock formations just behind Frank. "I think there's a drinkable spring not too far north and a little west of here," he said.

"But that's in the opposite direction of where we're heading," Joe said, letting out a sigh of impatience. "We were going east. I can't believe someone could get into our tents without our knowing it. Stupid, stupid mistake."

"It looks like they didn't leave a trace behind," Frank said, walking the perimeter of their campsite and checking for clues. "Not even a pebble's been disturbed."

The three packed in silence, gnawing on trail mix and dried fruit as they worked. Within minutes they were climbing back up the levels of rock, their packs snugly adjusted. Even in the early morning, the heat of the sun was intense, and the blue sky held no trace of the previous day's thunderstorm.

Kip set a blistering pace—it was obvious that he was angry and frustrated about his pack being broken into—and it took Frank and Joe a few minutes to work out the early-morning stiffness in their shoulders and backs. They had been hiking steadily for over an hour before Kip found the fresh spring. They stopped to boil as much water as they could carry. Once it had cooled they filled every container they had.

Frank could see Kip's anger fade once they were stocked with fresh water again. "It won't be easy to make do without the purification tablets,"

Kip said. "It's hard to find drinkable water, so we'll just have to ration what we have very carefully. But at least we have some."

"And we can get back to searching for Jorge," Joe said.

"Right," Kip said, pulling out his map again. "We can head southeast and get into Robbers Roost Canyon in about an hour," he said. "Just keep watching out for weird slots and cutoffs."

He folded the map again and set off down a particularly steep slope that required them to leap down to lower levels. Then they began to hike through more level country, weaving in and out of fantastic-shaped canyons, with towering walls and smooth, unusually curved rocks, worn down by years of wind and water.

In the midst of the spectacular scenery, Frank kept his eyes peeled for any sign of human presence. But the solitude was overwhelming. At times, it felt to him as if they were the first people ever to walk there.

Abruptly Kip stopped. They were in a narrow canyon, its walls looming high on either side. "It gets really narrow in through here," Kip said. "There's room enough for only one person to squeeze through at a time, so we'll have to go single file."

"There isn't any chance of getting stuck, is there?" Joe asked with a smile.

Kip laughed. "I've never seen it happen." He

led the way through the canyon, followed by the Hardys. Soon the walls were so close that Kip had to take off his pack, turn sideways, and sidle through, pulling his pack after him.

"Okay," he called to Frank. Frank could just see Kip through the sliver of light let in by the narrow passage. He dropped his own pack and worked his way through the canyon following Kip's example. The dull red rock drew right up to his face, feeling cool and moist. He took a deep breath and squeezed his way through.

As Frank emerged on the other side, he thought he could hear a rumbling sound above. At first he thought he was imagining it, but as it got louder, he realized it wasn't his imagination. Within seconds he felt a flurry of small rocks and stones pelting down on him. Shielding his forehead, he looked up and saw a huge boulder rolling down the sheer rock wall. It was headed straight for Joe, who was struggling to pull himself out of the narrow passageway.

"Avalanche!" Frank yelled as Kip covered his head with his arms. "Get out of there, Joe!"

Chapter

10

"HERE!" FRANK YELLED TO JOE. He leaped back toward the passageway and reached in. He felt around, grabbed Joe's arm, and pulled. Kip reached in, too, and they gave Joe a yank so that he burst through the end of the narrow passageway, falling in a heap at their feet.

There was a large crack, and the boulder crashed to a halt, wedging itself in the passageway, right where Joe's head had been seconds earlier.

Joe scrambled to his feet, and the three of them stumbled away, trying to shield their heads. Small rocks and pebbles continued to bounce down the path after them. Within about fifty feet, the canyon widened again, and the rain of rocks and dirt tapered off.

They turned to look cautiously back up the canyon to check if the avalanche was over. Just a few rocks and small stones were coming down the canyon toward them.

Joe turned to Kip and Frank. "Where did that come from?" he asked, his voice sounding quiet after the loud crashing of the rock slide.

Frank shook the dirt from his hair. "Out of nowhere," he said, peering up at the top of the hundred-foot rockface.

"That's right," Kip said, brushing the dust from his shirt. "It was a freak accident, but it's odd because this isn't an area where there should be any loose rocks or movement." He was squinting back up at the top of the canyon walls. "What soil there is, the rain yesterday should have packed."

"So maybe it wasn't an act of nature," Joe said.

Kip acted surprised. "You think Jorge could have started *that?*"

"Let's go check it out," Frank said. "Can we climb up to the top?"

Kip nodded. "When this canyon opens up, we can climb back around on an easy slope."

"That boulder came pretty close to smashing my head in," Joe said, lifting his battered-looking pack. "I'd like to find out who's trying to ruin my day. Especially if it's Jorge—after I risked my hide trying to save him from falling into those rapids."

Frank craned his neck, making one more sweep of the canyon walls. Kip knew this area as well as anyone, so Frank had to endorse his theory that the chances of that rock slide being a freak of nature were slim to none. So, was there someone up there now, watching them? Someone who was clever enough—and mad enough—to start an avalanche and almost crush his brother's skull.

Frank shook his head and followed Joe and Kip to the end of the canyon, where Kip began climbing to the top. The three hurried up the smooth rock surfaces in silence. They were moving fast now, propelled by the nervous energy brought on by the rock slide. It also felt good to be out of the narrow, claustrophobic canyon and back onto open ground.

When they reached the top, Frank was surprised to see that it wasn't a level stretch of rock but an uneven, rolling ledge. Parts of it were still wet from the rain, despite the bright sunshine that morning. There wasn't much to break up the landscape: The rock formations stood virtually alone, with just a few scraggly trees and bushes sticking up here and there.

Without speaking, the three of them fanned out across the ledge to search for clues as to what had started the landslide. The area to search wasn't large because they knew the slide had had to start just above the narrow canyon below. After a few minutes, Joe spoke up. "Well, this proves somebody's been up here, probably this morning."

Frank and Kip went over to Joe's spot on the ledge. There was a small depression in the rock just before it curved up to the edge and dropped off to the canyon a hundred feet below. Frank leaned over Joe, who was crouched just above the depression. "You can see the boot tracks," Joe said, pointing to the moist sand. "And there are skid marks here, too."

"You're right," Frank said, kicking some small loose stones with his foot. "Somebody was here, and it looks as if he was pushing something heavy over the ledge." He looked around the top of the rock. "But where would that person find a boulder that big and how would he move it?"

"Maybe over here," Kip said. He had walked several yards away to where a jagged tower of rock stuck up from the top. He kicked the bottom of it, and some pieces crumbled and fell away. "You can see where some of this soft stuff has already broken off."

Frank walked over to Kip, pointing down as he did. "And you can see a path of scratch marks on the rock from someone pushing another heavy rock over the edge."

"No question about it then," Joe said. "Somebody started that rock slide."

Frank was frowning. "I just don't see Jorge

doing that. The kid isn't that big, and he's got to be exhausted from being on the run."

"Have we seen anybody else since we got here?" Joe asked.

"The fact that we didn't see anyone could mean the person's just really good at hiding out," Frank said.

"Bryson?" Joe suggested.

"He's a possibility," Frank said.

"All I know is, somebody out there is after us," Kip said. "He went to the trouble of breaking into our camp last night, and he just tried to land that boulder on top of us. Are you guys sure you want to be out in the middle of the desert with this person—or persons? Maybe we ought to just head back to Moab and file a report."

Frank rubbed his sweaty forehead. "We can't just leave Jorge and whoever else is out here to kill each other or die of exposure."

"Knowing the cops are searching in the opposite direction, we should cover this area," Joe added.

"But what if it is Bryson, and what if he's armed?" Kip said.

"Then he's dangerous and we need to stop him," Joe said. "There are three of us, and you know this area better than most people."

Kip sighed and finally nodded. The three took a last look around for anything they might have missed, grabbed a drink of water and a quick meal of tortillas smeared with peanut butter, and headed back down the rockface and off to the east.

A couple of hours later, Kip found another fresh water source he remembered. It was tucked away in a cavernous formation, almost hidden by some tall, jagged red rocks. They refilled their canteens and bottles, which were more than half empty from the hot, tiring hike.

As they left the spring, Frank detected the traces of some boot marks in the sand. There was no way to tell if they matched the tracks they had found on the top of the rock earlier or to tell if they were Jorge's. They only knew that someone else—someone who was looking for water—had been in the area. As they walked away from the spring, Frank glanced back at the tracks, with a silent hope that they *were* Jorge's and that they were closing in on the teen.

But as the afternoon changed to evening, they hadn't caught another glimpse of Jorge. Although Frank tried to reassure himself that they must be close, he knew there was always the chance the kid had taken off in a completely different direction. Frank had to wonder how long they should keep up the hunt without any definite sign of their quarry. Then he reminded himself that *someone* was out there, and there was a pretty good chance that that someone was following them. If they kept their wits about them, they should eventually be able to flush whoever it was into the open.

Finally Kip pointed out a flat section of loose, sandy ground just in front of an overhanging ledge and suggested they stop and set up camp. He led Frank and Joe beneath the ledge, where the three of them were surprised to see some cavelike spaces naturally cut into the rock.

"Hey, this is a great spot," Joe said. The holes were warm and dry, protected from the elements, and, after a quick check, looked to have plenty of room and no trace of animals.

"As long as we set up the camp stove out in the open air, we should be fine," Kip said.

Kip cooked dinner, a spicy rice-and-beans dish, while Frank and Joe settled their gear under the ledge. As they sat down to eat in the increasingly chilly evening air, Joe said, "I know we'll be better protected tonight sleeping in that cave. But I think we should keep watch. I don't want anyone messing with our stuff again."

"Good idea," Kip said. Frank nodded, his mouth full of rice and beans.

"I'll take the first leg," Joe offered. "I'm not too tired."

"Fine," Frank said, swallowing. "I'll relieve Joe, and Kip, because you're usually up early anyway, you can take the third watch."

Kip nodded as he scraped the last of the beans and rice into their bowls. "Does that mean Joe has dishwashing duty?" he asked, lifting an eyebrow.

Joe sighed. "All right, all right, I guess it's my turn. Just don't get used to it. I don't do it very often."

"That's for sure," Frank said.

Half an hour later, Frank and Kip were crawling into their sleeping bags, ready for a few hours of solid rest. The last thing Frank remembered thinking was how amazingly quiet these canyons were at night. It was silence he could almost feel—and maybe if he listened carefully he could hear whoever was out there. . . .

It was still that quiet when Frank awoke in the dead of the night. He knew he must have slept for a few hours. Groggy, he wondered why Joe hadn't woken him up yet. Crawling from his bag, he quietly crept to the place where the overhanging ledge stopped and gave way to the canyon.

He squinted into the darkness, peering around the opening.

Joe was gone.

Frank hurried back to the cave. Joe's sleeping bag was untouched. Frank quickly shook Kip awake. "What is it?" he said sleepily.

"Joe's gone," Frank whispered. Kip hurriedly climbed out of his own bag. Then he followed Frank under the ledge and out into the canyon. The two walked in opposite directions, quickly searching the area around their camp, then came back together, both shaking their heads.

Kip nodded back toward the cave. Frank turned, realizing they hadn't looked into the other openings under the ledge. He walked into the first dark cavern to the left, then stopped abruptly.

Joe lay on the ground on his side, his hands tied behind his back. Above him, his back to Frank and Kip, stood the figure of a man holding a rifle.

As Frank and Kip watched, the man nudged Joe with the stock of the rifle. Joe refused to look at him.

"Hey!" Frank yelled, stepping into the cave.

The man instantly wheeled around and raised his rifle, leveling it at Frank. "Move any closer and I'll blow your head off," the gunman said.

Chapter

11

FRANK HEARD A GASP from Kip behind him. The gunman was Russ Hyrum.

Frank stopped cold and stared at the old rancher. Even in the darkness, he could see Hyrum's steely, dark eyes fixed on him. His mouth was set in the same determined line it had been the time they'd met him on the street in Moab. But now Frank could see that the older man's hands were shaking and his chest moved up and down in short breaths.

"Looks like your attitude's a little different now than it was a few days ago," Hyrum growled. "And your brother seems to have quieted down, too," he added. Frank could see Joe's eyes blink up at the back of Hyrum's head, but he kept quiet.

"What do you think you're doing out here?" Kip asked.

Frank could see a smile form on Hyrum's mouth.

"You think you're the only one who can find his way around, boy?" Hyrum said. "I know this area better than anyone. Only I don't pretend like it belongs to me," he added, gesturing with the rifle and glaring at Kip.

Frank stared at Hyrum. He doesn't want to shoot anybody, Frank thought. Pointing the gun at them seemed to make him more nervous than it made Frank or Joe.

Frank flicked his eyes at Joe. Then he took a step backward and raised his hands to Hyrum. "Look, put the gun down," he said easily. "Then we can talk."

Just as Hyrum turned to Frank, Joe swung his bound legs at Hyrum. With a grunt, he kicked the rifle from Hyrum's hand, sending it skidding across the cave floor toward Frank and Kip. Hyrum dove for the gun, but Frank snatched it up first.

Holding the rifle at his side, Frank said, "Okay, Hyrum, no more games."

"That's my rifle," Hyrum shot back angrily. "And I can have the three of you arrested for assault and for misuse of public lands." He blinked angrily, but he did back up farther into the cave.

Kip shook his head calmly. "No, you can't," he said. Then he walked over to Joe, bent down, and untied the ropes around his wrists and ankles.

Joe slowly got to his feet, stretching his shoulders. "You okay?" Frank asked.

Joe nodded. Then he jerked his head toward Hyrum. "Thanks to him, though, the back of my head is going to hurt for a while. He must have sneaked up behind me. Something just walloped me, and I blacked out for a minute. Next thing I knew, I was lying here with him pointing his rifle at me."

Frank turned to Hyrum. "How long have you been following us?" he said.

The older man's face was set in a scowl, and he said nothing.

"What are you going to do?" Kip asked. "Hole up here without your rifle? You might as well cooperate with us. You're outnumbered now, and after all the trouble you've caused me and my uncle, I'd just as soon take your supplies and leave you out here to rot."

Hyrum dug his hands in his jean pockets and looked at the ground. Then he took a breath. "All right, so I've been tailing you since you left Moab," he said. He glanced at Kip. "I thought you'd pick up on that, Mr. Wilderness Guide. Imagine, an old guy like me fooling you all this time."

"Why are you following us?" Joe asked. "What do you want from us?"

Again Hyrum stared at the ground. "Well," he finally said, "I was checking up on the Coleses' operation."

"And what else?" Kip asked. When Hyrum didn't answer, Kip reached over Frank, took the rifle, cocked it, and aimed it at Hyrum. "I've had about enough of your garbage, Hyrum," Kip said. "Either you tell us what else you're up to or I'll put you out of your misery—and mine."

Joe was surprised at Kip's fierceness, but he figured it was about time somebody got tough with the old coot.

"I said, *what else?*" Kip said, his jaw clenched. "You'd better start talking or I start shooting."

"All right, easy, boy," Hyrum said, holding up his hands. "I was going to see if I could mess up some petroglyphs so I could blame it on you. If I had the physical proof, I could get media attention. With enough bad publicity, maybe all your phony environmentalists would keep their noses out of Utah and their feet off our land," he finished, eyeing Frank and Joe.

Kip lowered the rifle and rubbed his eyes with one hand. "Unbelievable," he muttered. "So now that you've followed us, you see how we operate. We have respect for this land. We want to preserve it just as it is. But we think it should be used by anyone who's willing to act responsibly, not just because you've lived here for seventy years or because your great-grandfather took it from the Indians." Joe could see their friend was on a roll now, and he gave Frank a quick wink as Kip went on. "Hyrum, you ought to be man enough to admit that you were wrong about our operation, that we're both out for the same thing, which is responsible land use."

"All right, all right, I guess I could have been wrong," Hyrum said with a shrug. "And I guess I'm sorry. Anyway, kid, you've got the gun, so what else am I supposed to say?"

"You could tell us about that boulder you dropped on us today," Joe said.

Hyrum's face went blank. "I didn't drop any boulder on you. In fact, I was waiting to see what you guys would do to *me* next. After you stole one of my food packs."

Frank, Joe, and Kip looked at one another. "It wasn't us," Joe said. "We didn't even know you were here."

Hyrum squinted. "So who pushed me over a ledge, grabbed my pack, and ran away?"

Frank was frowning now. "Somebody stole your food pack?" he asked.

Hyrum nodded. "I guess he could have taken more. I mean, he sent me right over a ledge, and it took me a while to get back on my feet. He left the other stuff."

Frank looked at Joe. "Bryson?" he said. "He probably needs supplies."

"It could just as easily have been Malin," Joe said.

"I don't know about that," Frank said. "I doubt he'd be out here alone and short on supplies."

"You never know with a guy like that," Kip said.

Hyrum looked from Frank to Joe to Kip. "Malin? You mean Freddy Malin? And who's Bryson?"

Frank took a breath and then explained why the three of them were in Robbers Roost Canyon. Hyrum nodded, saying he was familiar with the Right Directions program.

As Frank described Bryson's escape and the police search, Hyrum narrowed his eyes. "Sounds to me like this boy's in some trouble," he said when Frank finished. "And it seems like you could use some more manpower. I'd be willing to help."

Frank, Joe, and Kip stared at the lean, older man in surprise. Finally Joe said, "Help us? Just a few minutes ago you had me tied up with a gun pointed at me."

Hyrum shrugged. "I know. But just a few minutes ago I thought the three of *you* were after *me*. Maybe if we're willing to trust each other, we can sort this mess out."

Kip let out a snort. Frank knew Kip would

have a hard time trusting Hyrum, and Frank wasn't so sure he could either. So maybe that's just why we should work with him, Frank thought. If they kept Hyrum close by, they could keep their eyes on him. Out on his own, they couldn't be sure what he'd be up to.

As if reading Frank's thoughts, Joe said to Hyrum, "You'll stick with us? You won't wander off on your own?"

Hyrum nodded. "Wouldn't want to. Somebody's already attacked me once. I can do without any more of that aggravation."

With a final look at Joe and Kip, Frank nodded. "Okay, we set out again tomorrow. And we all keep an extra eye out for company. I'll go on watch now. The rest of you get some sleep. Something tells me we're going to need it."

The four of them just stood there for a moment in the darkness of the cave. Then Frank, Joe, and Kip filed out and into the next cave, where their sleeping bags were laid out. Hyrum went to retrieve his gear and soon returned. He laid out his sleeping bag near the others.

Frank walked out beneath the ledge to take his lookout post. As the others settled down to rest, he peered out at the inky canyon, wondering who might be peering back at him.

The next morning Frank and Joe emerged from the cave into the bright sunlight. The sky, broken up by a few high clouds, was just as blue as it had been the day before. More surprising to Frank, though, was the sight of Kip and Russ Hyrum bent over a detailed map laid out on a rock, with Kip pointing out their route east. "Now, there's a piece of scenery we ought to photograph," Joe muttered.

After a light breakfast, it took only a few minutes for the four of them to pack up and be on their way. As they climbed among the dramatic rock formations, each was quiet, preoccupied with eyeing the tops of the rocks and any tracks on the ground. The sound of their feet crunching on the canyon floor seemed extraloud in the absence of any conversation.

Kip led the way between two large, square-cut rocks. The space between them formed a sort of doorway, opening into a broad, flat canyon, defined by high walls on four sides. "This is a box canyon," he said as the four walked through the doorway. "It's a fantastic natural formation, but finding your way in and out can be tricky."

"And they don't provide any cover," Hyrum added, blinking nervously as he surveyed the tops of the surrounding rocks.

The group had moved about fifty yards into the box canyon when a single loud popping noise shattered the silence. Frank, who was bringing up the rear, recognized it right away as a gunshot.

He saw a poof of feathers fly out from a hole in the sleeping bag rolled on top of Joe's backpack.

Instinctively, all four of them crouched down and scattered, searching for cover. Frank half ran, half crawled to a small cluster of rocks in front of the nearest canyon wall. As he ducked behind the largest boulder, he heard a sharp whizzing sound and a pinging. It was another bullet, glancing off the rock.

Kip and Joe dove behind Frank, who raised up to peer over the top of the boulder. Lying on the ground about twenty yards away was Russ Hyrum. Frank could see a red spot on one pant leg.

"The old man's hit," Joe said.

"The ricochet from that second bullet must have got him," Frank said between clenched teeth.

Joe dashed out from behind the rock, grabbed Hyrum, and dragged him back to the shelter of the rocks. The canyon was quiet again.

Using his pocketknife, Frank ripped Hyrum's right pant leg to just above the knee, where the torn flesh was still bleeding. Kip pulled the first aid kit from his pack as Frank applied pressure to the wound with a sterile wrap.

Hyrum was grimacing. "I think it'll be okay," he said in a raspy voice. "I got dropped off an ornery horse into a fence post once, and it hurt worse than this."

Frank nodded. "It looks like the bullet just grazed your leg. Luckily, it's not bleeding too badly."

Still breathing hard, Joe scanned the rockface directly across from the boulders where they were hidden. "The shots had to come from the top of that rock," he said. "He's probably still up there, taking aim."

"Can you see anybody?" Kip asked, sounding a little dazed.

"No," Joe said.

Frank had already scanned the canyon floor. Now, still crouching behind the boulder, he said, "I think our best bet is that outcropping to the left, the one with the scrub brush in front of it. It's got cover on all sides." The outcropping was about twenty-five yards away, and because it was up against the canyon wall, the gunman wouldn't be able to shoot down on them.

Hyrum pulled himself to a sitting position. "What kind of lunatic is out there anyway? As soon as one of you boys gets a glimpse of somebody up there, I can give him a good scare with my rifle."

"At this point," Frank said, his eyes trained ahead, "I want to keep him in front of us so we can protect ourselves. I don't want—"

He was cut off by the sound of another gunshot. It pinged off a rock about two feet from

Kip's head, taking a good-size chunk of sandstone with it.

Frank whirled around. "That one came from behind us," he said.

Joe spun around and looked back up at the wall behind them. "It's another gunman," he said. "We're caught in a cross fire, and we're right in his sights. We've got to move quick!"

Chapter

12

"ALL RIGHT, LET'S GO," Frank said. He and Joe
each tucked himself under one of Hyrum's arms
and helped him to his feet. Then they took off
at a run toward the larger outcropping of rocks.
Kip grabbed Hyrum's pack and raced after them.

Another shot rang out, striking the dust inches
from Frank's foot. Frank stumbled and fought to
keep his balance. Joe grabbed Hyrum and
dragged him toward the rocks, his bad leg sliding
along the ground.

Frank fell forward and half ran, half crawled
toward the outcropping, where Joe, Hyrum, and
Kip were just ducking behind the first rock. Tripping over the scattered pebbles, his knees
scraping the ground, Frank took a quick glance
over his shoulder.

At the top of the rock wall directly behind him, Frank made out the silhouette of a man with a rifle at his shoulder. He's aiming right at me, Frank thought, and this bullet has my name on it.

Another shot rang out.

Frank rolled to the ground. As he popped back up, his eyes peered through the dust to the top of the wall again. He just caught sight of a rifle-carrying figure leaping behind a rock. Without wasting a moment, Frank scrambled to his feet and sprinted the last few steps to the rock outcropping.

"Check it out," Joe said, pulling Frank in behind the rocks. Frank looked where Joe was pointing. On the far side of the box canyon, Frank saw a man running along the cliff edge. "It's the guy who fired the first two shots," Joe said. "It looks like he just fired that last shot right across the canyon at the other guy."

Frank whipped his head back around to the other side of the canyon. The second gunman was nowhere to be seen.

"We gotta get out of here," Hyrum said, wiping the sweat from the back of his neck. "This is a shooting gallery, and we're sitting ducks."

Kip had his back turned to the group, studying the rock formations that surrounded them. "I think I found an exit," he said, turning around. He pointed to the northeast corner of the box canyon. "See how there's kind of an arch over there in the corner? I think we can slip out under that arch and climb up to that ledge where we just saw the first gunman."

Joe turned to Hyrum. "Think you can make it?"

Hyrum nodded. "I'm sore, but the bleeding's almost stopped. I'll be fine."

"We've got about fifty yards in the open," Kip said. "Those guys are going to open fire again as soon as they see us."

"My guess is they're shooting at each other now," Joe said. "But even if they aren't, we don't have much choice. We're better off moving now before they have a chance to regroup."

The four of them readjusted their packs and, with a nod from Kip, took off running for the canyon corner. They were ready to duck for cover at the first sound of a gunshot, but there wasn't one.

They passed under the arch and turned left, climbing up the nearest rock. As their pace slowed, Frank could feel all of them relax, free from the confines of the box canyon. But Frank's own eyes shifted around warily, looking for any sign of either gunman. He had been too far away to get a good look at them, and all he could do was speculate. He just hoped one of them wasn't Jorge desperately shooting at the only people who could help him.

Within minutes, they were on top of the rock

where they had seen the first gunman. Frank stopped with a winded Russ Hyrum, checking the older man's leg wound while Hyrum took a long drink from his canteen. He could see Kip and Joe cautiously making their way among the scattered boulders.

"Somebody really ought to be watching our backs," Hyrum said, following Frank's line of vision. "Those riflemen could be anywhere—"

Suddenly Joe gave a holler. "Hey, look what I found over here." The other three went running over to where he was crouched down, holding a rifle in his hands.

"Careful with that thing," Hyrum said.

"It's not loaded," Joe answered. "I checked. We do have experience with firearms, Mr. Hyrum."

"Must be the one that first shooter used," Frank said.

"How do you know?" Hyrum said. "Maybe he had two. Maybe there's more than two of them."

"I do know it's warm and it's well oiled," Joe said. "Whoever shot it must have used up his ammo and dropped it on the run."

"The question is, where'd he run to?" Frank asked almost to himself as he scanned the surrounding, flat-topped rocks from their higher vantage point.

"Well, if he's hiding around here, it looks like he's minus a gun," Joe said.

"But the second guy still has one," Frank said.

"True," Joe said. "I'd say our safest bet is to go after the first guy to see if we can get him to tell us what's going on."

Kip had been staring out into the distance, where red rocks rose into the sky. Now he turned to Hyrum. "Isn't there an old mine around here?"

Hyrum nodded. "Yeah, there was a small uranium mine past this canyon and into the mountain. You think someone would hide there?"

Kip shrugged. "There's not going to be much cover in the small canyons around here. I'd head into the mountain area."

Frank and Joe looked at each other. "We might as well try it," Joe said. "It's better than getting caught in a canyon ambush again." The four of them loped back down the rock, following Kip as he led them across a large expanse of sand that gradually rose to an area of more hills and more vegetation. The climb became steeper and the terrain rockier as they hiked farther into the mountains.

Nearly an hour later Kip stopped on the incline, his shirt stained with sweat. "It should be right around the next bend," he said as they each took a quick drink of water. Finishing the incline, Kip approached a relatively flat area, which seemed to lead right into the mountain. As Frank caught up to him, Kip said, "This must be the place. There's—"

He stopped suddenly as Frank pulled up short. Frank was staring into the entrance of the old mine, a round black hole in the side of the mountain. And sitting right there on an old mine car was Freddy Malin.

Malin's eyes widened when he saw Frank and Kip. Then he quickly raised his arms in surrender. "Okay, I'm unarmed," he said, his voice oddly flat. "And I don't have anything you can take."

Joe and Hyrum joined Frank and Kip. "Malin," Joe said when he saw the Right Directions program director. "So you *have* been following Jorge—and us."

Malin stood up from the car as the four of them approached the entrance. His skin was covered with a layer of fine dirt, he looked tired and disheveled, and he had a black eye. "Yeah, of course I've been trying to find Jorge. He's in my program—he's my responsibility."

Kip let out a sarcastic laugh. "Is that how you deal with your runaways? By shooting at them?"

"Hey, I'm not shooting at anyone!" Malin exclaimed. "I'm the one being shot at."

"By whom?" Frank said.

"By that nut, Bryson," Malin said.

"Bryson's definitely out here?" Joe said. "You saw him?"

Malin sighed, rubbing his dirty shirtsleeve

across his face. "Who do you think it was shooting at you in that canyon before?" he said.

Eyeing Malin carefully, Frank pulled his canteen out and handed it to the smaller man. "So, exactly what's going on?" he asked.

"Oh, man, thanks," Malin said, tipping back the canteen and taking a long drink. He wiped his mouth and handed it back to Frank. Then he swallowed and looked around nervously. Finally he said, "Bryson found me yesterday. Well, I should say he ambushed me. He took my pack and beat me up pretty good, at least until I managed to get my hands on my rifle."

He paused, his sunburned cheeks getting even redder as he spoke. "We had a kind of standoff, Bryson with his rifle and me with mine. But I couldn't win. He had my food, my water, everything. So I had to hand over my ammunition. He forced me to try to lead him to Jorge. But then we saw you guys."

Frank nodded grimly. Now there was no question but that Jorge was a moving target out there.

"So now Bryson's after us, too," Joe said.

"That's right," Malin said. "He figures he has to get you guys out of the way or he won't be able to get to Jorge." He looked at the four of them. "Look, I didn't want to help the guy, but there wasn't much I could do. When he saw you go down into that box canyon back there, he figured he had you. He made me stay in one position from the top of the rock and fire a couple of shots into the canyon just to flush you out into the open so he could get a clean shot."

Frank looked at Malin. "But when he was about to take the shot at me, you shot at him from across the top on the other side?"

Malin nodded, his mouth drawn down in a thin, tired line. "I couldn't sit there and watch him kill you. I don't think I hit him, but at least he didn't get you." He looked at Hyrum. "Sorry about your leg."

"Thanks," Frank said to Malin. "I owe you."

Malin shrugged. "Well, we're probably all in trouble now. Bryson's one very angry man at this point. He's a tough cookie and not exactly level headed. Right now, he's got one thing on his mind and one thing only—revenge."

Frank turned to Joe, but before he could say a word, a shot rang out. The five of them whirled around, ducking instinctively. Down the mountain, a few hundred yards away, stood a figure with a rifle.

"It's Bryson again," Malin yelled out.

"Come on," Joe called. Crouching, he ran through the entrance of the mine into the dark tunnel ahead. Frank, Kip, Hyrum, and Malin followed him, crowding into the large, dank tunnel.

Joe pulled his penlight from his pocket and switched it on. It gave off a small shaft of light, the only thing visible in the darkness. Joe stopped for a moment, playing the light around the interior to get his bearings. He figured Bryson would charge right into the main tunnel after them.

The light revealed a smaller side tunnel just to their right. "This way," Joe said, his voice low. He led the way into the narrow passageway, his light playing on the wooden framework that reinforced the opening.

The others scrambled after Joe, with Frank bringing up the rear. A few seconds later, there was a rumbling sound from behind him, and Frank turned his head, half expecting to see Bryson. Behind him, the mountain was shaking itself to pieces. There was a sudden clacking of rocks and splattering of dirt. It built to a quick crescendo, then everything went still.

Frank stared at the pile of earth where the tunnel entrance had just been. The entrance was completely blocked off—they were trapped.

Chapter
13

FRANK CALLED AHEAD to the others in a level voice, "Hold up, guys."

The footsteps in front of him stopped. Now Frank saw a faint light play across his face as Joe hurried back down the tunnel toward him, leading with his penlight, the others following.

"The entrance caved in," Frank said, his voice a dull echo in the entombed space.

"This is it," Malin's voice called out from the darkness. "We're trapped."

"Easy," Russ Hyrum said, just in front of Frank. "Nobody's dead yet. You just stay calm."

"Anybody think there's a way out at the end of this tunnel?" Frank heard Kip ask.

"Doubtful," Hyrum said. "It's too small to be

a main artery. Probably just a secondary route. But we might head down a ways just to see."

Frank could see the shapes of the others in the tunnel as his eyes gradually adjusted to the darkness. Kip reached into his pack. "Here," he said to Joe. "Use my flashlight. It's bigger."

With the stronger beam bobbing ahead of him, Joe led the way down the narrow tunnel. Lined with packed earth, it was cool and quiet. Ahead of Joe, the flashlight picked up a straight pathway. They followed it until it ended in a solid wall of earth. Joe stopped, playing the light around. "This is it," he finally said. "There's no exit. This was probably from another cave-in years ago."

"Like I said, we're trapped," Malin said. "Bryson's got us just where he wants us. Buried alive."

Joe swung the light in Malin's face. "Well, what would you tell your students to do in this situation? Panic—or use their common sense and some teamwork?"

"He probably just wouldn't give them any food," Kip muttered, "then harrass them until they were mad enough to claw their way out with their fingernails."

Malin's eyes narrowed as he stared into the beam. "Sure, whatever you say, Kip. Why don't you just—"

Frank cut him off. "We should try to dig

through the fresh cave-in. It shouldn't be packed too hard."

"I agree," Kip said. "We don't have any picks or shovels, so we'll just have to do the best we can with our hands."

"Let's go," Hyrum said, leading the way back.

Joe propped the flashlight beam against one wall of the tunnel so that it illuminated the earth-and boulder-filled entrance. Then he and Frank, Kip, Hyrum, and a reluctant Freddy Malin began scooping away mounds of dirt. The muffled silence soon gave way to the sounds of grunts, labored breathing, and the smack of dirt and rocks being tossed back into the tunnel.

Frank picked up his rhythm as he thought about the advantage Bryson had. Now he could go after Jorge without interference and without witnesses. If Jorge was the one who had stolen the rifle from Ted Coles's office, there was a chance the armed teen might shoot if he became cornered. Then he could really get himself in trouble.

Frank looked up, panting. "Do you still have your cell phone?" he asked Kip.

Kip nodded. "It's in my pack."

"So let's call the Bureau of Land Management," Frank said. "Somebody out there should go after Bryson."

Kip shook his head. "It won't work in here," he said. "When we get out, I'll call."

With a nod, Frank went back to his digging, his fingernails thick with dirt and mud. He could feel an ache between his shoulder blades as he dug scoop after scoop. It wasn't long before Joe, heaving a large boulder aside, grunted, "There. I can see light."

The others crowded around Joe's quarter-size hole, staring excitedly at the faintly illuminated main tunnel on the other side. They doubled their efforts, scraping and pawing at the damp earth, bumping into one another as they worked furiously to carve out a crawl space.

It took another twenty minutes to widen the hole enough for a man to squeeze through. Frank watched as each of them pulled himself through the rubble, dragging his pack behind him. Frank was the last to climb out. "Careful, guys," Frank said. "We don't know where Bryson is."

They emerged cautiously from the mine, squinting in the bright sunlight. They searched the rocky spires and ledges for any sign of life, but it was deathly quiet all around.

Kip pulled some energy bars from his pack, handed them around, and said, "Now what?"

Frank frowned and pulled at his lower lip. "We've lost at least an hour on Bryson," he said. "I've got to believe he's out there and closing in on Jorge."

"So where would Jorge go?" Joe asked. "Before we can call the Bureau of Land Management, we have to figure out where to send them."

"Aren't we pretty close to the actual Robbers Roost?" Frank asked.

"Right," Kip said. "And to Silvertip Spring, which is where the Hole in the Wall Gang had a shoot-out with the law."

"I say we stick with the assumption that Jorge's following the Butch Cassidy trail," Frank said. "It's really the only reason I can see him coming out to this area."

"That's exactly what I was thinking when I came out here," Malin said. "He wouldn't know where else to go."

"Do you think Bryson knows Jorge's a Butch Cassidy fan?" Frank asked.

"My guess would be Jorge used to talk about it when he and Jeremy were running with him," Malin said. "Bryson doesn't know his way around the area. Lucky for him, I showed up and he could force me into being his tour guide."

"If he doesn't know his way around, he could be walking into an ambush set up by Jorge," Joe said.

"Good," Kip said. "He'll get what he deserves."

Frank frowned. "Hold it right there. We

wouldn't want Jorge doing anything he'll regret, would we?"

"I say we don't need any more shooting, period," Hyrum said. "Let's not waste any time. Robbers Roost is just down this hill and north into that dry, flat section just over there," he added, pointing northeast.

"You doing okay?" Kip asked Hyrum.

The old rancher nodded. "Just fine, and it'll be an easy hike anyway."

Kip made his phone call to the BLM, letting the rangers know where they were, where they were headed, and why. Then he took off and set a quick pace. Within minutes, they were moving across a more level, whitish gray area of desert rock and sand. Frank could see that everyone was continually scanning the expanse of land around them, squinting, even behind sunglasses, as the sun glinted off the white and red rocks. They hurried across the flats until they came to the mouth of a small canyon.

Kip stopped there, with Frank and Joe on either side of him. "I think we ought to split up," Frank said. "We've got to search the canyon, and we don't all want to get caught inside."

"The way we already did once," Hyrum said.

Joe nodded, wiping his forehead with his sleeve. "Kip, Hyrum, and I can take the eastern rim," he said to Frank. "You and Malin take this western side."

Frank turned to the others. "Just be careful. Use whatever natural cover's available and don't leave yourselves out in the open."

"All right, let's move out," Joe said. Frank watched his brother head off with Kip and Hyrum to climb to the top of the eastern rock. Then he and Malin started their trek up the western rim.

As Frank and Malin climbed, the landscape became cut with jagged outlays and dotted with scrawny juniper trees. Frank could hear Malin's labored breathing behind him. They came to a large rock that stuck out toward the edge of the canyon. Frank carefully made his way around it, gripping it with outstretched arms. He watched as Malin grabbed the same fingerholds and crept around the edge.

But as Frank came around the corner, he stopped suddenly. On the top of another ledge, about a hundred yards away, Jorge Robles was picking his way over the rough surface at a run. Scrambling after him, a rifle in his hand, was a short, wiry, bearded man.

"It's Bryson," Malin hissed behind him.

Frank barreled up the rock ledge, sprinting toward Jorge and Bryson with Malin right behind him. Frank's feet slid on the slick rock, but he caught himself with his hands, barely breaking stride. He watched Jorge slip because of the crumbling rock ledge, catching himself before more rock gave way.

"He can't keep his footing on that edge," Malin said.

Frank knew that, but he also knew Jorge would do anything to stay out of the open area back from the edge, where Bryson would have an easy shot at him.

Frank sprinted ahead, charging after Bryson. He made it up the incline and scampered across the rim. Bryson seemed to be gaining on Jorge, who was slipping and sliding all over. He must be tired, Frank thought. The teen was barely outrunning the older man, who was moving clumsily but fast.

Frank dashed to within twenty yards of Bryson. He knew if he could just get a little closer to the escaped con, he could take him down.

Then suddenly Jorge stumbled and missed the ledge altogether. Frank watched as the teen slipped over the edge and slid out of view.

Before Frank could react, Jorge grasped at the gnarled trunk of a small tree protruding from the sheer rockface. The trunk bent under Jorge's weight, but it held, and he dangled in midair.

Frank burst ahead as Jorge strained to pull himself up by the tree, but Bryson was there first.

His dark hair matted to his dirty face, Bryson leaned over the edge of the cliff to take a good look at Jorge. He wiped his hands on his jeans, slung the rifle over his shoulder, and pulled a big knife from a strap at his ankle.

Bending down, Bryson put the knife to the teen's arm. "I've been waiting a couple years for this," he said. "Say your prayers, Jorge."

Chapter

14

"STOP RIGHT THERE!" Frank yelled, his voice echoing through the small canyon. He charged along the cliff edge toward John Bryson.

Bryson popped up, whirled around, and pointed his knife at Frank.

Frank pulled up short, and Bryson stared at him with an intensity Frank had never seen.

"Back off, kid," he snapped at Frank. "I don't know who you are, but you'll be better off not seeing this."

Bryson's eyes were wide open and fearless; the muscles in his lean upper body were tensed and ready for action. His T-shirt was dusty and sweat stained, and there was several days' stubble covering his chin and lip line.

135

Frank met Bryson's malevolent stare and shook his head. "Too late, Bryson," he said.

Suddenly Bryson's eyes shifted to a spot just behind Frank. The corners of his mouth dropped. "Malin," he said under his breath. Then, louder, "I can't believe you have the nerve to show your face in front of me again, you gutless piece of slime."

Out of the corner of his eye, Frank watched as Jorge continued to pull himself up to the rock. The best Frank could do now was keep Bryson occupied to buy Jorge some time.

"Give it up, Bryson," Frank said. "Every law enforcement official in two states is looking for you."

Bryson turned back to Frank. "Thanks for the bulletin," he said. "What do you think? They have cops walking a beat in these canyons?"

"What do *you* think?" Frank shot back. "That you can try to kill Jeremy Reis and now Jorge here while everyone just stands around and doesn't lift a finger?"

Bryson stepped forward, jabbing the knife at Frank. "I know this much—*you're* not going to do anything about it." His eyes blinked at Malin. "And all the teenage backpackers in the world aren't going to protect you from me. I don't take kindly to my guide leaving me halfway through the trip."

As Bryson talked, Frank watched Jorge. The

teen had managed to pull himself back onto the rock. Now he was crouched quietly on the ledge where Bryson couldn't see him. Slowly he began to inch away.

"Hey, I did exactly what you asked," Malin protested. "You took my food and water and—"

"And then you shot at me," Bryson finished, leveling a hard stare at Malin.

"You—you didn't give me a choice," Malin stammered. "Did you expect me to—"

Suddenly there was a scraping sound from behind Bryson. As Bryson whirled around, Frank saw Jorge sprinting away, his arms churning and his backpack bouncing.

Frank heard Bryson grunt in surprise. Frank took a step forward, expecting Bryson to go after Jorge. But the short man turned back to Frank and Malin, snapped his knife shut, and returned it to his ankle strap in one fluid motion. Then he flipped the rifle off his shoulder, took aim at Malin, and, before Frank could react, fired off a shot.

The sound of the gunshot echoed off the canyon walls and Malin yelled, "Aahhhg!" Frank dropped to the ground, but Bryson had already spun back around and started after Jorge. Next to Frank, Malin had collapsed, and his breath was coming in short, quick gasps.

Frank turned to Malin, who was clutching his left shirtsleeve where a red stain was already spreading down his arm. His ears ringing from the rifle blast, Frank carefully lifted Malin's sleeve. The bullet had ripped through his upper arm, tearing away flesh but missing the bone. Malin's face was drained of color, and a low moan came from between his clenched teeth.

Frank helped Malin to a sitting position. Then he quickly tore a strip from the bottom of his T-shirt, applying it to Malin's wound to stanch the bleeding. "Oh, man," Malin said, wincing. "I thought he had me. I guess I'm lucky he didn't aim better."

Frank glanced back and forth from Malin's arm to the distant rockface, where Jorge and Bryson had run. Then he nodded at Malin. "Hold that cloth tight and make sure the bleeding stops. It's going to hurt, but I think you'll be okay." But I don't know about Jorge, Frank added to himself.

"That guy's crazy," Malin said almost in a whisper. "I don't think—"

He was cut off by the sound of footsteps slapping on the rock face behind him. Frank looked up to see Joe and Kip running toward them, Russ Hyrum jogging just behind them. "What happened?" Joe yelled. "We thought we heard a gunshot."

"You did," Malin said, nodding at his arm.

The three of them took a long look at Malin's blood-soaked sleeve. "Are you all right?" Kip asked.

"I think so," Malin said.

"The bullet just ripped through the flesh," Frank said. "It didn't go too deep."

Joe looked at Frank. "Bryson?"

Frank nodded. "We can't waste any time. Jorge got a head start, but Bryson's after him. And Bryson's not in any mood to talk," Frank said.

Joe looked down the rockface. "Did they head north?"

"Yeah," Frank said. He wriggled out of his backpack. "We'd better hurry up."

"Go ahead," Kip said. "Hyrum and I can stay here and watch Malin."

"Just keep Bryson in front of you," Hyrum added as Joe dropped his backpack.

Frank nodded, turning to run after Joe, who was already racing across the rock. Without his heavy pack, Frank felt as if he were flying. The brothers sprinted over the level surface at the top of the rock and then slowed a bit as they descended, ledge by ledge, into the area below.

They paused at the bottom. "Jorge wouldn't stay here in the open," Frank said, catching his breath.

Joe pointed up at a tall, narrow rock jutting up from the desert floor a few hundred yards ahead of them. "It's the only cover around here," he said between breaths.

Frank nodded, and the two of them took off

again. It took them less than a minute to reach the base of the steep rock. They slowed, and Frank could feel every nerve in his body come alive as they began to circle around the formation.

As they reached the back side of the conical rock, another, smaller rock came into view just behind the larger one. There was a narrow passageway between the two.

Frank whispered to Joe, "Let's not get stuck in here. We'll each take a side and search it from both openings."

Joe nodded and, without a word, turned back and began running around in the other direction. Frank waited for a minute to let Joe catch up and then headed into the passageway.

The two rocks towered above Frank on either side of the curved canyon. They were so close together that Frank could have touched them if he had spread his arms out. Instead, he kept close to the bigger rock, moving forward cautiously.

Coming around the bend, Frank stopped suddenly. Several feet ahead of him, backed against the wall of the smaller rock, was Jorge. He was staring in terror at something in front of him.

Frank drew himself up flat against the rock wall. He didn't want Jorge to see him because if Bryson had him cornered and the teen reacted, Bryson would probably start blasting away and ask questions later. Slowly Frank inched his way along the wall. He could hear somebody muttering, but he couldn't make out the words.

Moving along with his back to the wall, Frank looked across the canyon to see Joe, flattened against the opposite rock wall, still as a statue, watching Frank's side intently. Frank was relieved. Joe must have Bryson in his sights.

Frank silently moved a little farther along the sandy floor of the canyon. Again, he glanced over at Joe, who was still staring, immobile. Frank wondered why Joe wasn't giving him any kind of signal. As he inched forward to take a look around the corner, he stopped short.

Just a few feet away from him, in profile, was John Bryson. The escaped convict had his rifle raised to his shoulder. And he was pointing it directly at Jorge's head from inches away.

Chapter

15

FRANK KNEW THEY HAD just seconds to stop Bryson. The walls of the canyon seemed to close in as he stared at the man's profile.

A slight movement caught Frank's attention. Shifting his eyes, he saw Joe pick up a small rock, cock his arm, and wink at Frank. Then, with a flick of his wrist, Joe hurled the stone against the rock wall just behind Bryson. Frank watched Bryson spin to the right, pointing the rifle in Joe's direction.

At the same instant, Frank threw himself at Bryson, catching him in a flying tackle. He drove Bryson into the ground with a hard thud.

As Bryson fell, Joe ran to Jorge. The teen seemed to be paralyzed with fear, his eyes glued to Bryson. "Run!" Joe yelled. He shoved Jorge forward, nearly tripping over Bryson and Frank, and the terrified teenager ducked and sprinted away.

Joe turned back to where Frank and Bryson were locked in a vicious scuffle on the ground, kicking up a cloud of dirt and dust. Frank's hands were wrapped around Bryson's neck as he tried to hold the convict away from him. Bryson landed a few hard punches to Frank's midsection, then tried to struggle free.

Just as Joe was about to jump in, he noticed the rifle lying just a few feet away. He sidestepped Bryson and bent down to scoop up the gun.

Just then Bryson flung his right arm out, grasped the rifle, and swung it around toward Frank, his right index finger finding the trigger. Frank looked up to see the barrel of the rifle a couple of inches from his forehead.

This guy is strong, Frank thought as a foot came swinging through the air past his head. Joe's powerful kick sent the rifle flying from Bryson's hand. The blow stopped the convict long enough for Joe to leap on top of him.

Frank slithered from under Bryson and pinned his arms down.

"Okay, Joe," he said as Joe landed a hard left-right-left combination to Bryson's jaw. "I think we've got him now."

Huffing and puffing, Joe rolled off Bryson, who lay on the ground moaning, his face bloodied. "Hold him," Joe said to Frank. "I don't trust him."

Joe jumped up and jogged down the canyon. Jorge was sitting on a rock, scared and exhausted. "Come on," Joe said. "He's finished."

Jorge got up slowly, eyeing Joe with suspicion. But his exhaustion seemed to overcome his fear, and he followed Joe into the passageway.

A couple of minutes later Joe heard a whirring sound overhead. He looked up to see a police helicopter hovering above the narrow canyon. Joe looked back down at Frank with a grin. "I guess they finally decided to come west," he said.

Frank squinted up at the sky. "And it's about time."

Minutes later Frank and Joe led Bryson out of the narrow canyon and joined Kip, Malin, and Hyrum in the flat area just outside where the police helicopter had touched down. The cops from Moab had joined up with a couple of BLM officials, who had come by truck. Jorge was gratefully eating a tortilla Kip had offered him, staying as far from Bryson as possible, even though he was handcuffed in the back of the parked helicopter.

Frank took another long drink of water and

rubbed his midsection, which was a little sore from Bryson's pounding.

"Thanks, guys," Jorge said. "I guess I was wrong about you. You really were out to help me."

"I'm just glad you made it," Kip said. "After all this, it would have been a shame to lose you."

Jorge cast a doleful look at Malin. "Yeah, it looks like I can do this survival thing pretty good."

"So why did you run away from us when we saw you in Canyonlands when Jeremy was hurt?" Joe asked.

Jorge's expression was pained. "I shouldn't have done that. I shouldn't have left Jeremy. I guess I just panicked. I guess I thought I was going to get blamed for him being hurt." He suddenly looked up at the cops. "Is Jeremy going to be all right?"

One of the cops, a muscular man with slicked-back dark hair, nodded. "The hospital says his condition has stabilized."

Jorge nodded, looking relieved. He turned to Joe. "Jeremy went out to look for water that morning. When he didn't come back, I went looking for him. I had just found him, all beat up like that, when you guys saw us."

"So you never saw who attacked Jeremy?" Frank said.

Jorge shook his head. "I thought it might have

been him," he said, nodding at Malin. "Or somebody from the program. We knew they were already angry at us for complaining and fighting and running away."

"So you thought somebody from the program beat up Jeremy and that Malin would try to pin it on you," Frank said. "To protect yourself, you took some files from the Right Directions office."

Jorge nodded. "I needed some kind of proof that the program was holding back on our food and making us go on torture hikes, so I was looking for anything I could find in the office. I had it all in my diary, but I lost that."

"We've got it," Frank said.

"That's great," Jorge said, brightening. "So you *do* know. But I thought I didn't have any evidence and that if Jeremy died or something, I'd take the fall."

"So you took off, figuring you could hide in Robbers Roost," Joe put in.

Jorge shrugged. "Where else was I going to go?"

"How'd you manage to get all the way over here?" Frank said.

"Well, I guess I had a pretty good head start on you guys," Jorge said. "I hitchhiked, then I walked the last few miles."

Kip suddenly looked at Jorge. "So you were the one who broke into Uncle Ted's office to get supplies for your escape," he said. "But what did you do with the rifle?"

Jorge dropped his head for a minute. "Hey, I'm sorry about that. I just didn't think I could trust you guys. I'll replace everything. And the rifle—" He shook his head. "That was stupid. I took it, but then I decided I didn't want anything to do with a gun. I just dropped it in the desert after about a day."

"Bryson must have found it," Hyrum said.

Bryson stared back at them through the open door of the helicopter, his hard eyes expressionless. "Brilliant deduction," he said to Hyrum.

"And then he 'found' some water, too," Frank said. "That is, he stole it from our camp. When we caught up to him again, he started a rock slide and almost killed us."

"Bryson's the one who beat up Jeremy, not me," Malin said.

"No kidding," Joe said, rolling his eyes. "He would have got Jorge, too, if we hadn't stumbled on them. He had to make a run for it once the BLM and the hospital helicopter came."

Frank looked into the helicopter. "You went after Jeremy in the hospital, didn't you, Bryson?"

Bryson shrugged. "You know how many times I almost got killed in prison? Why should those two be out taking a vacation while I'm locked up paying for something they did?"

"Some vacation," Jorge said under his breath.

"So you put that note in Kip's truck," Joe said, staring at Bryson. "You went to the Right Directions office, too."

"Must have been right after me," Jorge said quietly, facing Bryson for the first time.

"Almost had you, too, punk," Bryson said. "I shouldn't have taken the time to write that note. I thought I could catch up to you, but I couldn't." He shrugged. "Lot of things I shouldn't have done. Instead of knocking those supports out of that old mine, I should have just shot all of you when you ran in there. Picked you off one by one."

"How about that frayed anchor?" Joe said. "We were rappeling down this slot canyon when we first got to Canyonlands and I almost bought it because my anchor rope was no good." He looked at Jorge. "What do you know about that?"

The teen shook his head and looked at Malin, who also shook his head. Joe looked at Hyrum, who just shrugged.

"Just like I explained, Joe," Kip said. "It was an old anchor that wasn't safe anymore."

"You mean Joe was in too much of a hurry to check that old rope?" Frank said, a smile starting to crease his face. "Gee, that's hard to believe."

Joe shot Frank a look.

The dark-haired cop nodded at Malin. "We'd better get that wound of yours looked at," he said. "And I think you have a few questions to answer, too."

Malin opened his mouth, looking as if he were going to protest again but then stopped. "Look, maybe some of my counselors got a little carried away." He shook his head, his face tense. "Maybe I did, too." He looked at Jorge. "I didn't mean to hurt anybody, just teach a few kids a thing or two about discipline and responsibility."

Jorge stared at Malin without saying a word.

"Hey, I did keep that nut from killing everybody," Malin said, his voice high with anxiety. "And I helped hunt him down, too. That ought to count for something."

"He's right," Frank said levelly. "He put himself in danger to help us."

The officer nodded. "We'll take that into account," he said. He looked over at Hyrum. "We should probably take a look at that leg of yours, too," he said, noting Hyrum's torn pants.

"You can look at it all you want," the old rancher said. "But I can tell you it'll be fine." He jerked his head toward Bryson. "That fool's got lousy aim."

Then Hyrum turned to Kip. "You were right. You fellows are okay. A kid would learn more on one of your tours than he would in any so-called survival program." He reached out and shook Kip's hand. "Don't forget to tell your uncle that his business will always be welcome in Moab if I have anything to say about it."

Kip shook Hyrum's hand with a smile. "Well, I don't think I'll be leading any groups in the near future. I'm planning on taking a little vacation before I go into any of these canyons again."

Frank gave a tired laugh as he and Joe turned to pile into the BLM truck with Kip and Jorge.

Kip turned to the Hardys. "By the way, gentlemen, there's no charge for this tour. And please, *don't* come again."

Frank and Joe's next case:

Irene Weinhardt's father, renowned physicist Kenneth Weinhardt, has been officially declared dead. But his body has never been found. When the Hardys agree to help Irene investigate her father's fate, they discover that his supersecret research into superconductors may have been worth millions . . . making him a select target for foul play! The search leads Frank and Joe from the famed laboratories at Los Alamos, New Mexico, to the frigid continent of Antarctica to the very frontiers of science. As the evidence mounts, it doesn't take an Einstein to see that this equation adds up to danger. And a shocking discovery in the ice could leave the boys out in the cold for good . . . in *Absolute Zero,* Case #121 in The Hardy Boys Casefiles™.